DUE DATE

FEB 2 4 1991			
AUG 1 2 1991			
DEC 8 7			
MAY 0 9 1996			
MAY 1 3 1997			

A Root

```
F          Hedberg, Nancy.
HED           A rooted sorrow.
#7062                                    $6.95
```

CHRIST UNITED METHODIST CHURCH
4488 POPLAR AVENUE
MEMPHIS, TENNESSEE 38117

Y0-CVA-808

A Rooted Sorrow

NANCY HEDBERG

Tyndale House Publishers, Inc.   Wheaton, Illinois

CHRIST UNITED METHODIST CHURCH
4488 POPLAR AVENUE
MEMPHIS, TENNESSEE 38117

Direct quotations from Scripture are taken from the *New American Standard Bible,* © The Lockman Foundation, 1960, 1962, 1963, 1968, 1971, 1972, 1973.

First printing, June 1987

Library of Congress Catalog Card Number 87-50006
ISBN 0-8423-5713-0
Copyright © by Nancy Hedberg
All rights reserved
Printed in the United States of America

Canst thou not minister to a mind diseased,
Pluck from the memory a rooted sorrow,
Raze out the written troubles of the brain,
And with some sweet oblivious antidote
Cleanse the stuffed bosom of that perilous stuff
Which weighs upon the heart?

WILLIAM SHAKESPEARE, *Macbeth*

CHAPTER 1

THE hay fields were bleached and dusty. Tractors and threshing machines crept through them, leaving behind paths of stubble and swarms of frantic grasshoppers. The steady hum of a tractor drifted through the open windows of the living room, mingling with the clink of punch glasses and the careful conversation of Milford's educators.

Although I had been raised on one of the farms surrounding the small college town of Milford, Oregon, the dry, dusty aroma of hay stubble no longer reminded me of harvest. Now, late August meant that Milford Junior College would once again gobble up Eliot, taking him away from me as surely as the threshing machines chopped down the heads of wheat and sucked them into their innards.

I had been watching Eliot from across the room. His tall, lean frame was erect with the discipline of a man who tended toward stoicism, but the effect was softened by his boyish mop of curly dark hair. He was talking to Sylvia. When we got home he would say, "That what's-her-name is sure something, isn't she?"

He could never remember their names.

I walked across the room toward them, and as I approached I heard Eliot say, "It only seems natural to cross-discipline some of the history and philosophy classes. You really can't teach one independently of the other."

Eliot and Sylvia were so engrossed in their conversation that for a minute I thought they were going to ignore me. But then Eliot looked up and said, "Oh, hi, honey."

"Hi. Hello, Sylvia."

"Hello, Rebecca. Your husband is quite the schemer. He's determined to get into my philosophy classes and bore my students with his dry, old chronicles."

"Oh, don't let Eliot hear you say things like that," I said. "The past is alive, don't you understand? Alive!" I spread my arms the way I'd seen Eliot do as he expounded on the importance of history.

Eliot turned his attention back to Sylvia. "Well, it is. Just think how much more interested your students would be in nineteenth-century philosophy, for instance, if they knew more about what was going on in the world at that time."

As he spoke, I studied Sylvia's tall, slim figure, her shirtwaist dress, and her simple pumps. Plain, very plain. But I had to admit the overall effect was striking. I glanced down at my strappy sandals and fidgeted with the bow on my blouse. It seemed puffy and frivolous.

Sylvia waved a perfectly manicured finger at Eliot. "Eliot, may I humbly quote just one such nineteenth-century philosopher?" She lifted her eyebrows delicately as she spoke. " 'Experience and history have taught that people and governments never have learned anything from history or acted on principles deduced from it.' "

"Nonsense. Who said that?"

"Georg Hegel." She managed to sound competent and helpless at the same time.

"Georg Hegel. I might have known. Well, if we've never learned anything from history, how can history teach us that we've never learned anything?" He scratched his head and then continued his argument, comparing the search for truth outside the context of history with a game of roulette.

When I walked away, Eliot shifted a few inches closer to Sylvia. Otherwise he gave no indication he noticed me leave. But Sylvia noticed. I knew Sylvia noticed.

"Oh, Rebecca, I've been looking all over for you. Where have you been?" It was my friend Marlene.

I nodded toward Eliot and Sylvia. "I was listening to Eliot convince

Sylvia they should cross-fertilize."

"Cross-fertilize!"

"Well, whatever they call it when they exchange class time."

"Oh, you mean cross-discipline." She tilted her head to one side and smiled her reproach. "Really, Rebecca. Cross-fertilize!"

I thought cross-fertilize was a witty way of putting it, and I was disappointed in Marlene's response. That was the trouble with Marlene—no sense of humor. I shrugged my shoulders. "Let's go get something to drink," I said.

We made our way across the spacious living room to the refreshment table. "I hope she's not serving Kool-Aid again," Marlene said. Marlene was a health food enthusiast.

"Nope. Hawaiian Punch."

"Hawaiian Punch! Yuck!"

"Your vocabulary rivals only that of the Cookie Monster," I said. "You've been watching too much 'Sesame Street.' "

But Marlene wasn't listening. She had picked up a cookie from the reception table and was examining it closely.

"Oatmeal," she said with approval. Roughage, she was thinking.

"Is Tom looking forward to the new school year?" I asked.

"Well, yes, but he taught summer school most of the summer so he hasn't had much of a break. He didn't even have much time to work in the yard this year."

"Hmm." Tom—master gardener, Sunday school teacher, purveyor of truth.

Marlene continued, "How did Eliot do on the remodeling? Did he get the bathroom finished?"

It was incredible the way Marlene managed to hit a sore spot every time she opened her mouth. I tried to keep my face expressionless as I replied. "No. He didn't get started."

"Didn't get started? He had all summer."

"I know." I started to make an excuse for Eliot but decided against it. I couldn't understand, either, why Eliot hadn't even begun when he had had the whole summer. "Maybe it was the expense," I said at last. "I think when he actually figured the cost he was a little overwhelmed. Maybe by next summer we'll be able to afford it."

"Well, I hope so. I don't know how you've put up with that bathroom all these years. He could at least fix the faucet. Your sink's getting so rusty."

I cleared my throat and frowned at my glass of punch. "You would think the wife of the college president could come up with something a little more exciting than Hawaiian Punch," I said.

"I don't care if it's exciting or not," Marlene said, "but all that sugar is just terrible for . . ."

I put my mind into neutral until she finished her "white poison" speech. When she was through, her gaze went past me to a newcomer across the room. "I wonder who that is," she said, nodding toward a dark-haired woman.

"I don't know. I noticed her earlier."

The woman was laughing, and as she tilted her head she ran her fingers through her long silken hair. Even from that distance I could see the sparkle in her eyes. Marlene narrowed her eyes. "She looks a little wanton, don't you think?"

I turned to the refreshment table. "Um," I said obscurely, hoping Marlene wouldn't require that I concur. I thought the woman was extremely attractive, but I hated to disagree with Marlene. She liked to gossip, and I tried to walk a thin line with her. If she thought the woman looked wanton and I disagreed with her, she might think I was wanton too. I imagined her presenting me as a prayer request at the women's Bible study. "I think maybe we should pray for Rebecca. I sense she's going though a . . . a difficult time."

We helped ourselves to more punch, then stood to one side again and sipped it as we observed old acquaintances and studied jittery newcomers. The President's Reception was an annual event, held in the fall to welcome new teachers and their spouses to the faculty of Milford Junior College.

"How do you feel about school starting?" I said.

"School starting? Oh, it will be nice to get the older girls back on a schedule. They've been so bored. But I'll miss having them home."

"You'll miss—? No, I mean Tom. Do you ever feel—?" I shrugged my shoulders.

"What?"

"I don't know. Never mind." Just then another friend of Marlene's joined us, and as they became absorbed in a discussion about the upcoming PTA election, I drifted back to the punch bowl. I poured myself another cup of punch and glanced across the room toward Eliot and Sylvia—Sylvia with the smooth hair and logical mind. Another history teacher had joined them, and the three of them were apparently transported into some bygone era.

The room was getting stuffy.

I passed Eliot and Sylvia on my way to the patio. Eliot was explaining the effect of the Norman Conquest on philosophy. I hurried past them onto the terrace, relieved to find it deserted. In the darkest corner I leaned against the railing, and though the evening air was warmer than I had expected, I still hugged my arms close to my body. For a moment I squeezed my eyes shut. The smell of the wheat harvest was still heavy in the air and, lonesome for my childhood, I was overcome with an unexpected wave of nostalgia.

Relaxing my arms, I leaned forward, my elbows resting on the top of the railing. Monday morning the Milford Junior College combine would grind into operation. Eliot would become bound in his other world like a bale of hay.

Sometimes I wondered what that world included. I'd read about sophisticated, intelligent women like Sylvia. Men seemed to admire the smart, logical types. Did they find them attractive as women? I wondered. Maybe they admired their fine minds as they would another man's.

This was Eliot's eighth year at Milford. I had been proud of him when he had accepted his first college position there. But the campus was not what I had envisioned. My idea of a college campus was Willamette University and its old ivy-covered brick buildings. At Willamette, huge spreading trees cast shadows on the lawn in the spring and littered the ground with leaves in the fall. The buildings had dignified names like Lausanne Hall and Eaton Hall. At Milford the buildings were numbered. Eliot's office was in Building 24, a rectangular module with thin partitioned walls. Strange that I could feel contempt for the college and still be threatened by it.

I shivered and went inside. Spotting the president's wife across the room, I realized I hadn't yet greeted her. I moved toward her.

"Rebecca," she said as I approached, "I was just telling Alison about you. Alison Willows, Rebecca Adamson."

So that was her name. Alison Willows. Her eyes sparkled even brighter at close range. We greeted each other, and I tried to tell from her expression what sort of things had been said about me.

"Rebecca," our hostess continued, "I was just telling Alison that I knew you two would get along famously. Alison's husband is a history professor too."

I wondered what her husband's teaching history had to do with whether or not Alison and I would get along. I studied her face more closely. She looked back at me with startling openness, her eyes dancing in amusement. Instinctively I knew my face had the wrong expression on it. I could feel my eyes; they were narrowed in tiny slits. When the president's wife was interrupted and had moved away, Alison said, "Don't you hate it when someone tells you you're going to hit it off?"

"Yes," I said after a surprised pause. "I always want to prove them wrong."

Wonderful, Rebecca. How to win friends and . . .

"Me too," Alison said, laughing.

I shrugged my shoulders. "Well, there isn't much hope for us then, is there?"

"Well, . . . we could become friends and not tell her." Her voice was filled with the intrigue of a woman used to creating her own mysteries—as if life didn't present her with enough questions to occupy her mind.

As she spoke I noticed she had several freckles on her nose, and I was pleased. I always trust women with freckles on their noses. It has something to do with Doris Day—she had all those freckles and would never go to bed with her leading men. That suited my moral code to a tee.

"Where are you from?" I asked.

"Illinois."

"Oh, Illinois," I said. I was ready to ask Alison the next question on my list of things to ask people when I don't know what to talk about, but Alison had a list of her own.

"Do you bake your own bread and check all the labels for BHT?" she asked without changing expression.

"Well, no, not always."

"Thank goodness," she said. "I don't bother with bread-bakers." I burst out laughing, but she continued. "Really. Women who bake their own bread are hopeless neurotics. They take out all their frustrations on a helpless piece of dough."

I covered my mouth. "That's terrible," I said. It really was an outlandish way to make an acquaintance. But I admired her audacity. I wished I could dispense with bread-bakers as easily. I always felt intimidated by them. Marlene was not only a bread-baker, but she could spot the letters *BHT* from the opposite end of Safeway.

Alison continued, "And have you ever noticed the people in the organic food markets? Most of them look like they need a good shot of BHT themselves."

Marlene's face came to mind. Her features did seem a little pinched. "Well," I said, "maybe that's why they're there. Maybe they just waited too long."

She wrinkled her freckled nose. "Maybe."

Those freckles. I stared at them and wondered again about Doris Day. Would Alison mess around?

No matter how hard I tried to reeducate myself, I knew my sense of morality was odd—or maybe just warped. I could tolerate lying, cheating, stealing, even murder, in some cases. But I never tolerated messing around.

"How do you take out your frustrations?" I said.

"What?"

"Your frustrations. You don't pound your fists into a pile of dough. What do you do?"

"Oh. Frustrations." She thought a moment. "Weeds. I'm a maniac about weeds." As Alison spoke I caught a glimpse of Eliot and Sylvia across the room. They were still engrossed in conversation, and I quickly turned back to Alison. "I snarl when I yank them. Dave says I grow instant fangs when I see them."

Fangs? For weeds? Alison's eyes shimmered and she wrinkled her freckled nose again, laughing at her own fanaticism. I pondered her freckles. Doris Day. Would she?

The question was off my lips before I could call it back.

"Do you mess around?" I said.

13

I'm sure the expression on her face was no more shocked than the one on mine. I had never in my life asked anyone such a question—not even my husband.

But she replied without hesitation.

"No."

"Good. Women who mess around are psychopaths."

It was her turn to burst out laughing.

We had reduced three months of getting acquainted to five minutes. We could become good friends, we both knew that, but neither of us knew if we wanted to. We spent the next fifteen minutes trying to catch up to where we already were. We asked each other the requisite questions—"How many children do you have?" and "Do you work?"

Out of the corner of my eye I noticed that Sylvia was leaving—walking smoothly to the door, her head held high. The reception had reached a lull—that point when people begin asking themselves if it's too early to leave. Eliot sidled over to say he was ready to go home.

I gave Alison our phone number, and she promised to call as soon as their telephone was installed. I genuinely hoped she would.

CHAPTER 2

OUR house was an old one, one of those monstrosities that line the main streets of little towns like Milford.

I loved it.

It had a front porch the width of the house, and there were two giant maple trees shading the front yard during the summer months. During winter the bare branches groaned in the wind and scraped across the roof with an eeriness that made being inside, close to the fireplace, wonderful.

The other houses along our street were impressive, with the awkward majesty of size, if not design. Most of them, like ours, had wide porches across the front.

We bought the house the year Eliot started teaching at the college. It had needed a lot of work, and we had attacked it with enthusiasm. We had gobbled our way down the list of remodeling projects until all that was left was the bathroom. That was two years ago. Work on the bathroom, as Marlene liked to remind me regularly, had not yet begun. Tom and Marlene lived two blocks away—in the suburbs, as Marlene put it.

When we arrived home after the reception, Eliot unlocked the front door and we both headed up the stairs to the children's bedrooms. We wanted to reassure ourselves that they were still there.

Shelly, our oldest, had just turned twelve, and we had recently started leaving the children home by themselves.

The light was still on in Shelly's room, but when I tiptoed in I found her fast asleep, an open book spread across her petite frame. She was lying flat on her back, one arm crooked on the pillow over her head. Her budding twelve-year-old body looked vulnerable and innocent in sleep. The boys slept on their stomachs, as if they were infants curling up into tiny balls, sucking their thumbs and clinging to the corners of their blankets. But Shelly had always slept on her back, her body sprawled in all directions, as if she had come into the world knowing she had a right to as much room as she needed.

I picked up the book and sighed. *Things Girls Should Know.* I hated to see her grow up, to have to come to terms with the world she had entered so self-confidently. I closed the book and placed it on the nightstand. After turning out the light, I tiptoed back into the hall and then into the boys' room.

It was dark except for the night-light, and in the semidarkness I stumbled over Matthew's pile of treasures. His rope wound itself around my ankle so that I had to kick it loose. Matthew's rope was a constant hazard. Sometimes it was coiled on the stairway, like a snake, and at other times it was strung across the room, one end tied to his bedpost, the other to the dresser knob. I had tried to get him to keep it in the garage, but he wouldn't hear of it.

Matthew had pulled his blankets into a hopeless tangle. He was wearing only his undershorts, and he looked as if he were desperately trying to keep warm. I straightened his covers, brushed the hair back from his eyes, and kissed him on the cheek.

On the floor next to his bed was his stack of joke books. Why didn't the child psychology texts warn you about jokes? They pointed out that ten-year-olds were active and forgetful, but did they ever think to warn you that by the time your child was twelve years old you would respond to any knocking noise by shouting, "Who's there?" and would then wait for some smart-aleck response?

Maybe Matthew was an extreme case.

Tyler's side of the room was much tidier than Matthew's. His teachers were going to love him. His books were stacked evenly on his nightstand, and his stuffed animals were lined according to height along the windowsill. He took turns sleeping with them. But he played favorites. Tonight was Straggles's turn again. He had to sleep with Straggles more than the others because Straggles had a bad self-image. He had a poor public image, too. I was always after Tyler about dragging that dirty, worn-out bear into the grocery stores and restaurants. It looked like a breeding place for germs—or vipers. But Tyler thought I was hurting Straggles's feelings.

I was trying to become more sensitive.

When I kissed Tyler's cheek, he murmured and smiled, integrating my kiss with his dreams.

I closed the door to the boys' room and walked down the hall, unzipping my dress on the way. By the time I reached our bedroom my dress had slipped down to my hips. As I stepped to the closet it slid to the floor and lay in a circle around my ankles. I stepped out of it, slipping off my shoes in the same motion.

Eliot was standing by the closet, meticulously straightening the creases in his trousers as he hung them on the hanger. He was still wearing his dress socks. Black socks and jockey shorts—I couldn't stand it. It was a joke between us. He knew I couldn't bear it when he took his dark socks off last. Once when we had finished making love, Eliot had leaped out of bed and pointed at his feet, laughing. He still had on his black socks. He thought it was very funny. I did too. That was one of the things that made me think our marriage would last forever—the fact that we both thought his making love to me while wearing his black socks was hilarious.

I put my robe on and sat down at the vanity. Before smearing my face with cleansing cream I leaned toward the mirror to inspect the tiny lines at the corners of my eyes. Then I moved away from the mirror and squinted my eyes, trying to decide if I really looked like Jane Fonda. A little, maybe—enough to make me keep an eye on Ms. Fonda's aging process, to see if I was ahead of her or behind her. I was pretty sure she was still ahead—she had a few more lines around the mouth. But I might be ahead around the eyes.

I watched Eliot line up his cowboy boots and wondered again why a college professor who leaned toward gray tweeds and somber wools insisted on wearing cowboy boots. His cowboy boots and his love of motorcycles were the major deviations in his otherwise integrated personality. And forgetting the names of women. He regularly forgot the names of women.

When he had straightened his boots, laid out clean underwear for the morning, set his alarm, and placed his briefcase by the door—making sure the snaps were facing the right direction—he climbed into bed.

"Are you glad school's starting again?" I said, as I slid into bed beside him.

"Um. I suppose so." He turned out the light.

"I wanted to talk."

"We can talk."

"But you turned out the light."

"I'm listening."

"You know I can't talk in the dark."

"That's silly. I never have understood that."

"You might go to sleep and I wouldn't know it."

"Hmm."

I could tell he already had his eyes closed and wasn't really listening. I was surprised by choking anger.

"You seemed to find a lot to talk about with Sylvia tonight."

I hadn't meant to bring up Sylvia. I was afraid he might actually enjoy talking about her, and I didn't want to give him the pleasure.

"That's her name—Sylvia."

"You knew her name."

"I couldn't think of it."

I didn't know whether to believe him or not. He really did have a funny thing about names. He never called me Rebecca. It was always *honey, dear,* or something like that. Sometimes he just called me *wife.* "Hi, wife," he would say. His sister Marcella was always *sister.* "Why don't we have *sister* and her family up for Thanksgiving?"

I resented sharing this little quirk with Sylvia and all the others. He should either call me by my own name and forget theirs, or the other way around. I heard Eliot's even breathing and realized he was nearly asleep already. I turned my back to him in irritation.

He sensed it. "Night, honey," he murmured in a sleepy, placating tone.

I closed my eyes and listened to the numbers change on the digital clock. *Click, slide, hum. Click, slide, hum.*

Sylvia and Eliot standing together on the other side of the spacious front room. Sylvia looking neat and attractive—stimulating. Eliot leaning toward her as she spoke. Nodding his head, his mouth slightly ajar . . .

The numbers on the clock continued to change discreetly. *Click, slide, hum. Click, slide, hum.*

Lying there, I remembered sipping coffee and nibbling on a cinnamon roll at my women's Bible study. Martha, our leader, was saying, "Don't forget that the women our husbands meet in the working world are not only often well-informed and stimulating, but they make a consistent effort to look neat and attractive. If our husbands come home and find us with our hair in rollers, unable to talk about anything but Johnny's new tooth and ring-around-the-collar, how can we expect them to love us the way Christ loves the Church?"

I took a sip of coffee and laid my cinnamon roll carefully on my napkin. "But doesn't Christ love us no matter what? Rollers and all?" I asked. Several women chuckled, but nobody said anything. "I mean, if our husbands are supposed to love us like . . ."

Martha's smile stopped me. It was her most patient smile, the kind worn by a mother whose child has said something innocently amusing. "But they don't, do they?" she said.

"Well, maybe not, but it says they're supposed to."

The eyes of the other women were fastened on me, and the atmosphere tensed. It went without saying that a happy marriage was the most important thing in the world to all of us, and most of us agreed that submission was an important ingredient in that marriage. It was a favorite topic of discussion.

"But, Rebecca, we cannot be responsible for our husband's obedience, only our own." She raised her trim eyebrows slightly. "Don't you agree?"

I took another sip of coffee and gave what I hoped would pass for a nod. Inside, I was indignant. It all seemed so pat, and left everything up to the wife. *What about mutual submission?* I wondered. The wife sets the temperature in the home. How many times had I heard that one? I stirred more cream into my lukewarm coffee. I happened to know that when Eliot came home scowling and dark, the thermostat in our house went completely bonkers.

"Besides," Marlene interjected, "for me, it's not just a duty, but a joy. I'm happy meeting Tom's needs and desires, even if it's just a small task like ironing his shorts."

I must have made a noise because Marlene looked at me strangely. Neither slave nor free, male nor female . . .

Click, slide, hum. Click, slide, hum.

I thought of our Sunday school class. "Hurry up, wife, we're going to be late," Eliot was saying. We slipped into two vacant chairs in the back row. Marlene's husband, Tom, was standing in front of our Sunday school class, open Bible in hand. "No woman will be truly fulfilled until she can submit to her husband," he said. He illustrated his point with a story about a child who became ill. The husband and wife disagreed over which physician to call, and Tom insisted they should call the one the husband chose. "Even if that child died, the wife shouldn't point out that her choice of a doctor might have saved his life."

I shifted in my chair. To me, his story illustrated that a spouse shouldn't say, "I told you so," not that the wife ought to submit. Several people coughed.

Tom continued. "If wives don't make efforts to fit into their husbands' plans, their marriages will be out of balance and contrary to the divine pattern. The woman was made for the man. The Bible makes it clear in 1 Corinthians 7:34 that the wife should center her life around her husband's plans, interests, and problems."

I automatically flipped to the passage in 1 Corinthians and ran my finger down the column of chapter seven. "And the woman who is unmarried, and the virgin, is concerned about the things of the Lord, that she may be holy both in body and spirit; but one who is married is concerned about the things of the world, how she may please her husband." I stared at the words. *Unmarried . . . concerned about the things of the Lord. Married . . . concerned about world . . . husband.* I read the words again to make sure I hadn't missed something. Still staring at the words, I raised my hand. No one noticed.

Tom said, "Let's bow for a word of prayer." He paused briefly. "Dear Father, we thank you for your divine order. Help us to understand that just as we, the Church, are subject to you, so our wives are to be subject to us. Dear Lord, help us as husbands to accept the tremendous responsibility and this divine order you have ordained. In Jesus' precious name, amen."

I opened my eyes and stared at the Bible still open on my lap. I read the words again and glanced around expecting someone to say something. But those around me were already making their way to the door. Marlene was rushing toward Tom. "That was great, Tom!" she said, her eyes aglow with pride.

"Are you coming, honey?" Eliot said.

"Oh, yes," I said. I closed my Bible but remained seated.

"Come on, honey. What's wrong with you?"

"Huh? Oh, nothing."

Nothing. Nothing. Sorry. Nothing . . .

Click, slide, hum. Click, slide, hum.

A thought of Alison burst into my sleepy future. Wilson? Williams? Willows. Yes, Alison Willows . . . *I invited her to sit at my kitchen table. But when we sat down Marlene was already there, her face a wavy smile. I asked Alison if she would like a cup of coffee. Marlene suggested we have herb tea instead. Alison insisted on coffee—black. I fixed tea for Marlene and coffee for Alison. I put the sugar bowl on the table and Marlene asked if she couldn't please have honey instead. I wiped off my sticky plastic honey bear and placed it on the table. What about me? I looked from Alison to Marlene with my uncertain Jane Fonda smile. Their faces were undulating like reflections in a distorted mirror. I poured myself a cup of coffee and squirted in some honey. Coffee to please Alison . . . honey to please Marlene . . . awful . . .*

Click, slide, hum.

CHAPTER 3

THE next morning Eliot left for the college early. He had stumbled around the bedroom, dolefully listing all the things he had to get done before school started. "What are you doing today?" he had asked on one of his passes by my side of the bed.

"I think I'll run out to the folks," I said. "Mother called yesterday and said Dad had had a bad day."

"Sorry to hear that."

"And I need to finish getting the kids ready for school. Tyler needs a lunch box."

"Uh-huh."

THRESHING machines and combines were chopping their way through the fields on either side of the highway as the kids and I drove out to my parents' farm. The grain blew gracefully in the wind in front of the reapers, but the stubble stood stiff and exposed where they'd already traveled. There were clouds of dust behind the machines, and the morning air, already warm with the coming heat, carried the dry, dusty aroma of harvest through our open car windows.

I enjoyed the short drive through the country to my parents' farm, but a darkness had crept over the farm itself—an uncertainty. The doctors had decided not to operate after all. Their explanation had been brief. Mother was upset with them because they wouldn't explain things so she could understand.

"Who's taking care of Grandpa's fields, Mom?" Shelly asked.

"He leased them out this year. I think to Mr. Bellows."

"What will happen if he dies?"

"Shelly, don't . . . I'm not sure, Shelly. We don't need to worry about that now."

MOTHER'S face was tired and strained when she greeted us at the door.

"How is he?" I asked.

"About the same. Hi, kids. There are some cookies in the cookie jar."

"Have you talked to the doctor since I talked to you?"

Mother shook her head as we walked into the kitchen. My three hungry offspring were jostling each other to be first in line at the cookie jar. I was sure one of them would knock it on the floor and break it.

"Hey, take it easy!" I said. "Why don't you guys go in and say hi to Grandpa and then run outside to play?"

"Come along, kids," Mother said. "I told Grandpa you were coming. He's eager to see you. But settle down, OK? He gets tired easily."

I turned on the unit under the teakettle and then glanced into the living room. The children were standing around Dad's chair uneasily, trying to be cheerful and solemn at the same time. Dad smiled at them, nodding his head, asking them vague questions, not seeming to care whether or not they answered him.

He didn't look good.

I stepped back from the doorway and stared around the little kitchen as I waited for the water to boil. It suited Mother perfectly—tiny provincial print wallpaper on the walls and ruffled white curtains at the window. Dad had never made as much money as he'd hoped—

and time was running out—but Mother had always managed to keep the house pleasant. It always smelled like Ivory soap. The whole house. I'd never understood that. A plaster-of-paris plaque on the wall said, "Only one life, 'twill soon be past, only what's done for Christ will last." There were plaques everywhere. "The family that prays together stays together."

They'd have to sell the farm someday. It was only logical.

Steam burst through the spout of the teakettle with a shrill whistle, and I hastily moved it to the next unit. They couldn't keep the farm forever. It was an awful thought. Other people living in our house, thinking it was theirs. Other kids walking through my fields and climbing my trees. But not the apple tree. Surely not my apple tree with its wide limb that branched into a generous V, just big enough to sit in and study the sky through filtering green leaves. No, it would always be my tree. You can't sell trees. Not really. They're like people. You can't sell people either. They've tried. The slaves. Plantation owners thought they were buying them. But the slaves knew better. Deep inside they knew they weren't possessions. And wives. An African chief trading three good oxen for a healthy wife. The wives knew better. They knew they weren't just so much merchandise. Didn't they?

"You'd better go see him while he's still awake," Mother said, as she handed another cookie to each of the children and shushed them outside. "He's going to lie down for a nap."

Dad was propped up in his chair next to the open window. The flimsy curtains rose and fell in the morning breeze. When Dad saw me he lifted his arm in greeting. "Hi, Becky," he said.

"How are you feeling?"

"OK."

"Everyone else is working their heads off." I smiled. "You should be ashamed of yourself. Harvey Bellows is out there on his combine choking on dust while you're lying around here being lazy."

Dad grinned, but his words were croaky and slow. "I was out talking to Harvey day before yesterday. He told me I deserved a little rest."

I nodded my head.

"Is Eliot here?" He glanced at the door as he spoke.

"No, he's at the college. School starts Monday. You know how he is at the beginning of the school year. He's convinced he'll never be ready for classes to start. You'd think by now he'd know it will all get done, one way or another."

"Serious. Too serious."

"He's all right."

"School starting again. So soon."

"They're all in school this year, Dad. Tyler starts first grade."

"You'll get lonesome." His eyes turned toward the window. As the curtain lifted and fell we could catch glimpses of the golden wheat in the field adjacent to our farm. "Mom got awfully lonesome when you and Susan started school," he said. "Awfully lonesome." He shook his head.

"Mom did?"

Dad nodded. Then he leaned his head back and closed his eyes. I decided I had stayed long enough. "I'd better go, Dad," I said. "You need to get some rest." I leaned forward, my hand on his shoulder, and kissed him on the forehead. "Don't give Mom a bad time," I said. "Behave yourself."

"I'm good to her. I've always been good to her."

"I don't know . . ." I straightened my back and looked at him with mock severity. But the eyes that peered back at me were serious, not filled with amusement as I had expected.

"I always tried to treat her right."

I pressed my fingers gently into his shoulder. "I know, Dad. I know." He tried. I guess they all tried.

I returned to the kitchen and fixed myself another cup of coffee. I told Mom to sit down for a few minutes. She was fussing around by the stove, doing heaven knows what. She plopped into a chair, but she looked awkward, sitting there, doing nothing. She hardly ever sat still.

"He looks terrible," I said. "How long has he been like that?"

Mother's fingers fluttered about her face aimlessly. "Oh, that man," she said. "I don't know what I'm going to do with him. Thursday he insisted on going out for a walk. I offered to go with him, but he said no, he kind of wanted to be by himself. I thought he was just going into the backyard to look at the flowers. He never goes very far. But when he didn't come back inside I went out to look for him." Mother shook her head slowly. "I should have insisted on going with him, I guess. He was clear over in that wheat field talking to Harvey Bellows. Harvey saw him stumbling across the field in a cloud of dust. He stopped the tractor and asked him what he was doing out there all by himself, and Dad told him he just wanted to see his farm again. He told Harvey not to run the place into the ground."

Mother brushed her fingers across her cheeks and shook her head. "Oh, Rebecca, he was so weak it was all I could do to get him back to the house. Harvey had to help me." Mother waved toward the living room. "He's been like that ever since."

"When did you take him to the doctor—after that?"

"Yes. But—those doctors." Her face clouded with anger. I guess it was anger—the murky, helpless anger of someone reconciled to impotency. "They don't tell you anything."

I shook my head. I preferred not to speculate on the doctor's silence, so I changed the subject. We discussed Mr. Bellows and the coming harvest. Then we talked about my sister Susan—when in the world she and Lance were going to start a family.

Finally, I drained the last of the coffee from my cup and pushed back my chair. "I guess I should round up the kids," I said. "We still have a few things to do before school starts."

AS I walked from the house to the apple orchard in search of the children I inhaled deeply, breathing in the aroma of harvest and the memories of childhood. I made my way through the orchard toward my favorite tree and enjoyed the feel of dirt clods crumbling beneath the soles of my sandals. Some of the dirt slipped inside, and it even felt good there, where it didn't belong, filtering between my toes and sifting between the straps of my shoes.

I couldn't hear the children's voices. They weren't in the orchard. They were probably in the barn. I continued walking toward my tree. I would look in the barn later.

My tree was still there, as self-possessed and proud as ever. I looked up at my wide limb with its gentle, spreading V and contemplated climbing up to my favorite spot. It seemed higher than I remembered. I settled for pressing my face against the scratchy bark. I held my cheek against the tree trunk and concentrated on the texture of the wood against my skin.

Closing my eyes, I tried to imagine what it was going to be like with all the kids in school . . . *All I saw was myself against a stark white background, my arms hanging limp at my sides—long arms, all out of proportion, long, limp, and heavy, my fingernails nearly touching the ground. I noticed that my fingernails were slender and carefully manicured, bright with red polish. It intrigued me to know that once the children were all in school my nails would be long and I would polish them red.*

Long red nails.

Long, heavy, idle arms.

CHAPTER

4

I HAD expected the first few weeks of school to be as hectic for Eliot as they always were, but this year he was even more harried than usual. At the last minute Sylvia Weston, the philosophy professor—the one whose name he couldn't remember—agreed to cross-discipline some of her classes with his. Eliot had spent hours altering his lesson plans.

He was still tense and jumpy when September ended. October arrived with a hint of frost, and the leaves across the valley turned from green to gold.

Eliot wasn't exactly depressed, just preoccupied. He always seemed to have one foot in another world, and I was more careful than usual to gauge his moods.

"LET'S GO," he said briskly one evening as we were getting ready to go out to dinner. He was pacing back and forth across the room as I hurriedly spread clear polish on my fingernails. I held my hand out and studied the pale nails. *I should get a bottle of Coral Flame or Raspberry Ice*, I thought, *so I can have red fingernails—like Sylvia.*

"I'm almost ready," I said, trying to keep my voice pleasant. It had been my idea to go out to dinner, and I knew that in his mood, any irritation could set Eliot off. "Let's just forget it," he would say in that tone I dreaded—dark and intense.

When I had asked Eliot if we could go out to dinner, he had opened his pocket calendar and glanced at it. "How about the twelfth?"

"Great."

October 12. Wife—dinner.

He had charted me into his schedule like a workout at the YMCA—he knew it was good for him, but he didn't expect to enjoy it.

I was still swishing my hands back and forth to dry my nail polish as we made our way down the sidewalk. I walked around to my side of the car and waited for Eliot to open the door. His right leg was halfway inside the car when he realized I was still standing beside my door.

"Oh, honestly," he said. He retrieved his leg and walked around to my side and opened the door.

"Thank you."

"You're welcome."

Eliot drove to the restaurant in silence. Lately Eliot always drove in silence. He drove in silence, ate in silence, and made love in silence. Several times I had tried to talk to him while he was watching television and had been asked to be quiet—during a commercial.

Once inside the restaurant, Eliot perused his menu with the same deliberation he gave his history books. As he studied the menu I studied his face. His eyelids drooped slightly at the corners, giving him a thoughtful, though forlorn, look. When he lifted his eyes from the menu and looked into mine, I was aware again of that strange something that had always drawn me to him—a look akin to pain. It tugged at me. I wanted to say, "I understand, I understand." But I didn't understand at all.

But if I was drawn to the pain in his eyes, I was also addicted to the shaft of light that shot through them on those rare occasions I was able to make the pain disappear. That was a joy I lived for—that shaft of light in Eliot's eyes.

The waitress approached and took our order. For a few minutes we chatted about the kids and Eliot's new students. But when she returned with our salads, we began eating in silence. Eliot concentrated on his food and ate rapidly. I poked around in the lettuce leaves, searching for something interesting, like a mushroom or a slice of cucumber. I jabbed my fork into a cherry tomato and chewed it in slow motion as I stared out the window. I wrinkled my forehead, laid down my fork, and rested my chin in my hand. "What do you think of Tom's Sunday school class?" I asked. "You know, all this stuff about wives submitting, and fitting in with their husband's plans—all of that."

Eliot narrowed his eyes slightly as he looked at me. "It's all right. Tom's not exactly creative in his teaching methods. Why do you ask?"

"Oh, I don't know."

"Hmm." He looked at me for a moment and went back to his salad.

I continued to poke at my plate. I stirred my fork round and round, finally spearing it into a tiny slice of radish.

"He said something that still really bugs me."

"Oh? When?"

I stabbed a cucumber slice. "A few months ago. He used a verse completely out of context. It still really bugs me."

"Good grief, honey. A couple of months ago? Why are you stewing about something that happened a couple of months ago?"

"Because it makes me mad, that's why. People who teach ought to at least know what they're talking about. He is either illiterate or he was deliberately distorting that verse—in which case," I said, shaking my fork at Eliot, "he ought to be drawn and quartered."

"Let's not be rash."

"Well, he did make me mad."

"Which verse was it?"

"That one in Corinthians about wives doing things to please their husbands. He used it to back up his point that wives should center their lives around their husbands. That verse is really explaining that because wives will be trying to please their husbands, they won't have as much time to concentrate on the work of the Lord. It's not a command to center their lives around their husbands—it's saying that married people have to give attention to each other, attention they could otherwise give to God. It's almost a recommendation to stay single."

"Well, I don't think the Apostle Paul was really recommending—"

"That's beside the point. The point is, the way Tom used it was totally misleading."

"Well, it's easy to accidentally say something you don't really mean when you're in front of a classroom."

"I don't think it was accidental."

"Well, maybe not. But don't let it bother you. Tom's really not a Bible scholar to begin with. Besides, it does seem like there are other Scriptures to support his point."

"What other Scriptures?"

"I don't know, they're there."

We ate the rest of our meal in silence. I had wanted to continue our discussion about Tom's class. I was particularly interested in those other Scripture verses Eliot had mentioned.

I don't know, they're there.

But it seemed senseless to pursue the discussion. Eliot's voice had been edged with irritation. It wasn't possible to converse with Eliot when he used that tone. Had I always known that? Or was I just realizing that Eliot could intimidate me by using his irritated voice?

CHAPTER 5

I LAY in bed with my eyes closed, listening to Eliot singing in the shower. When I heard him coming back up the stairs, I pulled the covers over my head and kept track of him with my ears. I heard the squeak of his belt as he drew it through the buckle, and his quiet grunt when he pulled on his boots. His footsteps came toward the bed and I squeezed my eyes together to screen out the light flooding my face as he pulled back the covers.

"Bye, Becca," he said, kissing me lightly on the forehead. "If Sylvia calls about the faculty meeting tell her it's at 4:30." He playfully nipped the tip of my earlobe with his fingertips, something he'd never done before, and turned toward the door. He stopped in the doorway. "OK, Becca?" Then he was gone.

I pulled the covers back over my head and clamped my hands over my ears.

Becca?

I closed my eyes and tried to go back to sleep, but I couldn't. Although it was a regular workday for Eliot, the children had no school—teachers' in-service—and I had wanted to sleep late. But sleep, the blessed peacemaker, and I could not reach a settlement. Instead, a small guerrilla force of fear skulked back and forth across my brain. I pressed my face into my pillow, trying to halt the advance. *Becca. Becca.* When had Eliot started calling me Becca? After all those years of being dear, wife, and honey, why had he suddenly started calling me by my name? Well, not my name, exactly, but close. Close. I had always thought I would love it. Instead I was filled with panic.

I glanced at the digital clock by the bed—8:32. The exactness of the numbers contrasted with the vagueness of my plans. From downstairs I heard the repeated violence of the cartoons and knew the children were up. I squeezed my eyes shut again and thought I remembered hearing the refrigerator door opening and closing. Opening and closing. The children must have fixed breakfast for themselves. I pulled the blankets closer to my neck and opened one eye, studying the sky through the sheer white curtains. Cloudless.

Finally, realizing I was expending more energy trying to stay asleep than I would by getting up, I pushed the covers aside and slipped my legs over the side of the bed. Without looking at the floor I slid my feet back and forth until I found my slippers.

I put on my robe and, walking down the stairs, I combed my hair with my fingers, drawing them from my scalp to the ends until my hair was fluffy and my scalp felt awake.

At the bottom I rested my elbows on the banister post. Shelly was draped across the couch, one leg hanging over the end. She had her beautiful blonde hair pulled into a strange new hairdo, and I could tell she'd been experimenting with eye shadow again. Matthew was sprawled on the floor wearing only his undershorts. I smiled at his uninhibitedness. He was unlike Eliot in every way. He had his rope tied to the curtain rod, creating a pulley apparatus. Tyler sat cross-legged next to Matthew, his eyes glued to the television, a faraway look in his eyes. He was wearing his Spider Man pajamas. They were the feet-in genre, but the feet had been cut off long ago and the ragged bottoms fell just below his knees.

"Did you have breakfast?"

"Umbledegrumph," they said without moving their eyes from the TV screen. I shuffled into the kitchen to fix myself a cup of coffee.

Pale, soggy Cheerios floated in the milk left in the children's cereal bowls, and a carton of milk sat on the counter, getting warm. I put the milk in the refrigerator and turned on the unit under my copper teakettle. As I walked from the refrigerator to the stove, sugar crunched beneath my slippers. I brought my teeth together in a grimace. Sugar on the floor always irritated me.

As I waited for the water to boil, I leaned against the counter and closed my eyes. I tried to imagine what the perfect mother would do with her children on a no-school day. When my coffee was ready, I took it into the living room and plopped on the couch next to Shelly. "How about driving up to Silver Creek Falls?" I asked.

Nobody answered.

But then, after the Roadrunner disappeared into the sunset, Matthew turned around and said, "Silver Creek Falls? Hey, neat, let's go."

THE rustic sign read "Silver Creek Falls State Park." The peak tourist season was over, and the parking lot was nearly deserted. I pulled into a spot close to the head of the trail.

There were rock walls along the path at the top of the falls that I always imagined had been built during the depression by the CCC or whatever it was called. I had no idea if that were true and couldn't imagine where I had gotten the idea, but I liked it. Eliot had always said I had a sense for history.

The children led the way down the slippery trail circling the main falls. "Be careful," I shouted, "it's slippery. Matthew, hold Tyler's hand."

As we got closer the cascade of falling water drowned out our voices and I watched the children in pantomime. Matthew and Tyler beat their chests like Tarzan as the spray from the falls spread its wetness through their hair and over their clothes.

I pulled the hood of my raincoat around my head and stuffed my hands into my pockets as I walked behind the sheet of water. The mist dripped down my face and the roar of the falls engulfed me.

Eliot and I had taken this same trail on a Sunday afternoon the summer before we were married. . . . *We stopped behind the falls and Eliot took me in his arms. We pressed our bodies hard against each other, filled with longing. And I started crying, crying with longing and anticipation and fear—fear that the oneness I longed for would never come to be. The spray from the falls covered our clothes and our hair, washing the tears from my cheeks.* . . .

Too soon, I was on the other side of the falls. I left behind a bittersweet moment of joy—today forgotten in yesterday, a reprieve from the assault going on inside my head.

Becca, Becca. If Sylvia calls about the faculty meeting tell her it's at 4:30. OK, Becca? "Re-becca. My name is Re-becca." *If Sylvia calls. OK, Becca?*

I pushed the hood back and brushed my fingers through my hair, checking the wetness. The path was no longer slippery, and I relaxed as I followed the children along the trail that led to the lower falls. The ground beneath the firs was carpeted with yellow and red leaves from the maples and birches that interspersed themselves among the evergreens. September and October had been arid months, so the leaves were curled and dry.

The children kicked the leaves into the air and watched them flutter back down to the ground. The rains would come in two or three weeks and then the leaves would cover the earth like a wet collage, slick and soggy.

I tried to remember how long the trail was around the lower falls. I glanced at my watch. We couldn't possibly get home before 5:30. Good. I would miss Eliot's call—his almost daily call saying he would be late for dinner. I imagined the phone ringing in the empty house. It pleased me to know I would not be there to answer the phone. Eliot would wonder where I was.

Or would he?

Maybe not. Maybe he would just sigh in relief and . . . and what? My mind came to a screeching halt and would not go on. I tried to force it on, force myself to think about Eliot and what he had been doing lately at the college, when in other days he would have been home eating dinner with his family. I forced my mind into his office. *When I didn't see him at his desk the room began spinning around me. I thought maybe I saw his shadow in the corner, and then a lightning flash of red fingernails, but the room was spinning too fast for me to be sure. I escaped into the hall, but the hall was whirling too, and my mind reeled from one wall to the other—the staggering of a drunk person. Imaginary doorways opened on either side, but when I tried to look inside, the rooms were dark and filled with shadows I was afraid to examine. I stumbled out of the building and into the parking lot to see if his car was there. But just before I got there I veered between the administration building and the library and sneaked into a narrow passage behind the stairs. I saw myself crouched there, on my haunches, behind the stairs, my hands pressed close to my ears, my eyes shut tightly.*

Everyone was getting tired.

"My legs hurt, Mommy. Please carry me."

"Tyler, I can't carry you. You're much too big. It's not much farther, you'll see."

But it took much longer to hike around the falls than I had anticipated. By the time we reached the car it was getting dark. It was nearly six when we stopped at the A & W Drive-In in Silverton for hamburgers. I called home from the phone booth on the corner. There was no answer. Late again.

As soon as our order came I started the engine and pulled back onto the highway. I held the steering wheel with my elbows as I unwrapped my hamburger. A glob of ketchup dropped to my lap and in the darkness I couldn't see where it landed. I held my hamburger in one hand and fished around for a napkin. I slid my bare hand cautiously across my thigh until I felt a soggy glob of ketchup sliding through my fingers.

"Oh, yuck," I said, resuming my search for a napkin.

Matthew leaned over the front seat. "Mom?"

"Matthew, how many times do I have to tell you not to pull on the seat?"

"Sorry. Mom?"

"What?"

"Do you know what you call a man who steals ham?"

"Hmm?"

"Do you know what you call a man who steals ham?"

I couldn't figure out why Eliot hadn't answered the phone. He should have been home by now.

"Do you?"

"Do I what, Matthew?"

"Know what you call a man who steals ham?"

"No."

"A hamburglar."

He waited for me to laugh.

"It's a joke, Mom. Don't you get it? A hamburglar. Don't you get it?"

"Oh," I said. "I get it now. A hamburglar." I faked a laugh. Matthew disappeared once again into the backseat.

The darkness had swallowed the surrounding landscape. I watched for the headlights of oncoming cars and concentrated on the yellow line that twisted its way through the countryside. Because of the unfamiliarity of the road and the awkwardness of trying to finish my hamburger, I was driving slower than usual. Matthew leaned forward and pulled on the seat again.

"Matthew—"

"Sorry, Mom. Mom?"

"What?"

"Do you know what confuses a man more than anything else?"

"No, what?"

"Driving behind a woman who does everything right."

"Matthew—"

"What?"

"Was that a joke?"

"Yep."

"I didn't think it was funny."

"Dad did."

"You're pulling on the seat again, Matthew. Please sit back."

"Sorry, Mom."

WHEN we arrived home, Eliot's car was in the driveway but the house was dark. I opened the front door. Eliot was on the couch, watching television.

"Where've you guys been?" he asked. "I called home to let you know I'd be a little late and there wasn't any answer."

"We went to Silver Creek."

"Hmm." Eliot had turned back to the television.

"I hope you weren't worried."

Eliot laughed. He was watching an old "I Love Lucy" show. "What? What did you say, Becca?"

CHAPTER

6

THE branches of the maple tree outside our bedroom window were stripped of leaves, and the taupe limbs were outlined in charcoal shadows as I studied the crisscrossed patterns against the blue winter sky. It was Friday morning, and I tried to remember if we had anything planned for that evening. It was unusual to have a Friday night clear, but I couldn't think of anything.

In an attempt to bring Eliot out of his shell, I had been trying to do something special for him each week. Not that he had noticed. Lately it seemed like he never noticed. But I wasn't about to give up. Tonight seemed like the perfect evening to have a candlelight dinner just for the two of us.

After planning the menu, I got it into my head that nothing but bright gold daffodils would do for the centerpiece. I called both of the florists in Milford. Neither of them had daffodils. I was not certain, in fact, that it was possible to get daffodils in December. But when I called several florists in Salem I finally found one that actually said they had dozens of fresh daffodils. I decided that when the kids got home from school I would take them to Salem for hamburgers, picking up the flowers on the way home.

When the children arrived home they drifted into the kitchen looking for something to eat. I was in the midst of preparing the Sunshine Sauce for the Lemon Mist Dessert. *Beat the eggs just enough to blend,* it said. Just enough. How much was just enough?

"Listen, you guys," I said, "just skip a snack today. In a little bit I'm going to take you into Salem for hamburgers."

"McDonald's! McDonald's! Can we go to McDonald's?" Tyler screamed.

"Tyler," I said, raising my voice, "you don't have to yell."

Place over gently simmering water. Gently simmering. I concentrated on the water bubbling in the saucepan. Was that gently simmering or moderately simmering?

"Mom," Matthew said.

"What?" I was still watching the water and my voice was loud with exasperation.

"When was radio first mentioned in the Bible?"

"Radio? In the Bible?" It had to be a joke. "I don't know. When?"

"When the Lord took a rib from Adam and made a loud speaker."

"I don't think that's funny, Matthew," I said. I made sure my voice was soft. "Why don't you go watch cartoons for awhile?"

Beat constantly with a rotary beater until mixture thickens, eight to ten minutes. I plunged the beater into the creamy yellow sauce and set the timer for eight minutes.

In came Shelly. "Look at my new yell, Mom. We made up new motions." She shoved the table against the wall and I turned sideways so I could keep one eye on her and one eye on the sauce.

"Milford Cougars
Rah rah, rah rah rah
Rah rah, rah rah rah
Rah rah, rah rah rah
Ye-e-e-ah, Milford!"

She did the yell full volume, just as if she were in the gymnasium. Her movements were jerky.

"How do you like it?"

"Fine. You need a little more practice though. But it's fine. It's a nice yell." I noticed some lumps forming in the sauce. I turned down the heat, lifting the top of the double boiler to check if the water was still boiling gently.

"This is our new victory yell," Shelly said. "V-I-C-T . . . Mom, you're not watching."

"Just a minute, Shelly, something's going wrong here." I rechecked the gently boiling water and turned the handle of the rotary beater as fast as I could. "Darn." Round and round the handle went in a furious blur. The number of lumps seemed to dwindle.

Matthew had returned to the kitchen and was leaning against the refrigerator. "Mom," he said, "who's the best doctor in the Bible?"

I wrinkled my brow. Jesus? Too spiritual? I chanced it. "Jesus?" I said.

"Nope."

There they were again. Tiny little pearl-like lumps. I turned the handle faster. "Luke?" I said.

"Nope."

This time they weren't going away. Lumpy Sunshine Sauce.

"Who, Mom? Who do you think?"

"I don't know, Matthew." My voice had turned shrill. "How should I know?"

Matthew remained unperturbed. Leaning against the refrigerator he fixed his eyes on me and said evenly, "Job." He paused dramatically. "He had the most patience."

"Matthew," I said between clenched teeth, "please get out of the kitchen."

LUMPY Sunshine Sauce.

By the time Eliot arrived home the children and I had returned from Salem. Eliot walked through the kitchen, his steps brisk, his hair slightly disheveled. He said hello to me, but his eyes just missed meeting mine. They darted past me to the next room.

"Eliot—"

"Hi, honey. I'm sorry—I don't have much time," he said. "I'm going to be late."

"Late?"

"Yes, very late, in fact."

"For what?"

I followed him up the stairs. His voice was irritated. "For the faculty meeting."

"You didn't tell me you had a faculty meeting tonight."

"I told you yesterday, on the phone. Remember?"

"You did not." I recognized the shrill tone in my voice again.

"Yes, I'm sure I did. I told you about it last week, too."

I searched my mind but couldn't remember anything about a faculty meeting. "Well, why didn't you remind me this morning? I fixed—"

"I didn't think it was my job to remind you of every little thing."

"Well—"

"Have you seen my blue sweater?"

"Oh—I think it's in the dirty clothes. Your green—"

"Oh, shoot. I was hoping to wear it tonight."

"Aren't you going to have time for dinner?"

"Nope, not tonight. I told you I have that faculty meeting."

"But—"

"After that I have to go over some curriculum recommendations with the philosophy department."

"The philosophy department?"

"You know, you know. That cross-discipline stuff." He slipped on a beige sweater and changed his boots.

"Hmm."

He turned to face me. "What do you mean, 'Hmm'?"

"Oh, nothing. Nothing. It's just that I had a nice dinner planned."

"Well, I'm just not going to have time to eat. I'll grab a hamburger after the meeting if I'm hungry."

He brushed my cheek lightly with a quick kiss and was gone.

After Eliot left I sat down on the bed and cried. Tears of frustration and disappointment coursed down my cheeks, leaving my eyes red and puffy.

But later as I sat at the kitchen table alone, eating my Lemon Mist Dessert with its lumpy Sunshine Sauce, I turned angry. I clenched my hands into fists and pressed them against my temples. I was so angry I didn't know what to do with myself. Suddenly I grabbed the dish of Lemon Mist Dessert and aimed it at the sink. The spoon went flying across the kitchen and the dish smashed against the sink, shattering the bowl and taking a neat chip out of the porcelain.

I wanted to roar out my anguish. I wanted to groan and heave out of myself the aching, angry constriction in my chest. But then I heard the sporadic canned laughter of "The Brady Bunch" coming from the television in the living room. The children. I stifled my desire to scream and dropped my head onto my arms. I sobbed quietly against the tabletop.

Later on, I managed to pull myself together enough to get the children to bed. Then I ran hot water into our claw-footed bathtub and dumped in enough bubble bath to make the water frothy with bubbles. Stepping into the white bubbles, I spread a washcloth across the end of the tub to keep my back from getting cold, and lay back in the tub. I piled bubbles over my body so I wouldn't have to look at it. I needed to think, and naked bodies distracted me.

What was I doing wrong? No matter what I said or did, Eliot seemed to be finding me irritating—an annoying infringement on his peace of mind, like a fly landing on your nose when you're trying to read. What was going through his mind lately? Was there some irritating flaw in me that I wasn't seeing? All I wanted was to make him happy—to keep us both happy.

I lay a long time in the bathtub, thinking of ways to improve my relationship with Eliot. I didn't know what I could do except what I'd already been doing. I'd just have to renew my efforts, that was all. I decided I'd just have to try harder.

The water had turned cold, so I hopped out of the tub. As I dried myself vigorously, rubbing the towel across my skin to erase the goose bumps caused by the cool bath water, I planned my strategy. Perhaps Eliot needed acceptance and admiration. I was going to try to be what he wanted me to be. I would anticipate his every wish. Things would eventually get better. They'd have to. Someday soon he would no longer drag home late for dinner. No longer would I have to shift from foot to foot while he charmed Sylvia and all his nameless students. He would have eyes only for me—because I was going to be perfect. Really perfect. I would be perfect and he would love me and cherish me.

Eliot was not going to know what hit him.

CHAPTER 7

IN the weeks that followed, one thing proved true—Eliot did not know what hit him. He did not, in fact, realize anything had hit him at all. He continued to eat, drive, and make love in near silence. But I kept trying to be the perfect wife, hoping that some day it would all start paying off.

Experience had taught me that people who say "I'll call you sometime" seldom do. So I was surprised to answer the phone one morning and hear Alison Willows's voice on the other end.

"Rebecca? This is Alison—Alison Willows, remember? We met at the President's Reception."

"Oh, right, right. Goodness, that was months ago. How have you been? Are you settled and moved in and everything?"

"Oh, it's been ghastly, you just can't imagine. I'd have called long ago, but it's been one thing after another. It seemed like I spent weeks waiting around for the electricians and telephone hooker-uppers to get their act together. They won't tell you when they're coming, you know. They assume women at home have nothing better to do than sit around and wait for them."

"Watching soap operas and eating bonbons."

"Exactly—exactly!" Alison laughed. "Listen, I'm going nuts around here. I still haven't met very many of my neighbors. Could we get together sometime?"

Normally I guarded my privacy like the gods surrounding a sacred burial ground, so I was surprised to hear myself inviting her over for a cup of coffee.

"Really? You mean right now?"

"Sure. Come on over."

The moment I hung up the phone I regretted my hasty invitation. It wasn't that I didn't want to see Alison. I did. In fact, I was pleased that she had called. Still, I hesitated. I wasn't sure Alison was a Christian, and I avoided non-Christians whenever possible. It wasn't that I was prejudiced; it was just that I had taken a personal evangelism class that I'd never recovered from. Within three months I had learned forty Bible verses to zap on people who were not born again. Since I wasn't very proficient at zapping people, the responsibility hung around my neck like an albatross.

Shortly after Alison arrived she planted herself in front of our bookshelves and scanned the titles.

"Are you a Christian?" she asked with the same openness I'd noticed at the reception in August.

"Uh, yes," I replied. Her question was understandable. Except for Eliot's history books, almost every book on our shelves had *God*, *Holy Spirit*, *Jesus*, or *Bible* in the title. There were a few subtle ones like *In His Steps*, which might have thrown a person if she didn't know whose steps it meant, but that didn't throw Alison.

"That's one of the better books on the Christian walk," she said, tapping the end of the book lightly with her fingertip.

"Oh, you've read it?" My voice was edged in relief.

"Yes, a long time ago."

"Are you . . . are you a Christian too?"

"Yes," she said, smiling. "I am."

I don't think I would have guessed. She didn't dress or talk like most of the Christians I knew. Everything about her was too—I don't know—loose, I guess. Her dark hair fell in loose waves to her shoulders, and her clothes hung on her with a freedom that was both casual and sophisticated. Even her walk was loose, a little self-conscious, maybe, but pleasantly so—pleasantly and self-consciously loose. When she talked, her face was open and she looked directly into my eyes. I felt I could have asked her any outlandish question and she would have answered it honestly. Then I remembered that at our first meeting I had done just that.

As I watched Alison browsing through our books I felt the same easy camaraderie of that evening months before. "How can you be a Christian?" I said. "You don't bake your own bread."

"If you will recall," she said, without missing a beat, "I don't mess around either. Besides, I said I was a Christian—I didn't say I was sanctified."

I laughed. "Come into the kitchen. I'll fix us some coffee."

We sat at the kitchen table and chatted about how Alison's children were adapting to the new schools and how Dave liked his job at Milford.

"What do you think of Dr. Satter retiring?" Alison asked as she brushed some crumbs from breakfast to the middle of the table.

"Dr. Satter? I didn't know he was retiring."

"You didn't? Next year. Dave says the history department is in quite a turmoil. There's even a chance Eliot could become head of the department. I'm surprised he hasn't said anything."

"Eliot's very modest," I said. But I too was surprised he hadn't said anything. Maybe that explained his preoccupation. Head of the department? Eliot? "When will they decide?"

"Sometime after the first of the year. Dave said March at the latest." Alison took a sip of her coffee. "But, yes, Dave likes his job fine. They all seem to be getting along great—Dave and the kids. I'm the only one having a hard time adjusting."

"You don't like Milford?"

"I don't know. A town's a town, I guess. It just seems like I haven't met very many people. Well, I meet people, it's just that nothing seems to happen after I meet them. We never get together or anything."

I shifted in my chair. I probably should have tried to contact her after the President's Reception. I probably should have done that. "Hey," I said, "maybe you'd like my women's Bible study. You might find friends there."

"A women's Bible study? I don't know if I could handle another women's Bible study."

"What do you mean?"

"Well, . . . " She rubbed her index finger lightly across her lower lip as she stared across the room. "Well, OK," she said. "What are you studying?"

I scratched my head. "It's kind of a topical study. We've been talking about the role of Christian women—finding fulfillment as wives and mothers—that sort of thing."

As I finished my sentence, Alison pressed her forehead with the palm of her hand. "Augh," she said, "I think I'm going to throw up."

"Alison!"

"Rebecca, I am sick and tired of hearing how to be a sweet, loving wife. It seems like every women's Bible study group on the face of the earth at one time or another studies about how wives can be more submissive to their husbands. The truth is, Dave is bored to death with me when I'm 'sweet and loving.' "

"Don't you think you need to submit to Dave?"

"I believe in Christian submission."

"There's a difference?"

"One is based on your relationship to Christ—how you view yourself before God. The other is based on your sex—I'm just a poor, helpless woman sort of thing."

"Well, I don't know that submitting is that bad," I said. "After all, it's a biblical principle. I don't think women are going to find fulfillment by trying to fit into a leadership role created for men."

"What do you mean, 'created for men'? Created by whom?"

"Well . . ." I noticed I hadn't put quite enough cream in my coffee. I walked to the refrigerator and added a smidgen more. "Created by God," I said as I closed the refrigerator door. "I believe God wants a married woman to be fulfilled in her role as wife and mother. It is the role of the man to be protector and provider." I was quoting word for word from one of Martha's lectures, but I thought it sounded pretty convincing.

"You don't really believe that."

"What do you mean?"

"You don't really believe that. You're trying to, you think you should—but you don't really."

"What makes you say that?"

"Rebecca, when we first met we hadn't talked two minutes before you said something . . . I don't remember what it was, but I knew it was the truth—what you really felt. But this—this role stuff—you don't believe it."

I cleared my throat. "Alison, I'm a Christian. I believe . . ." I squinted my eyes at her. "What do you believe?"

"Well, I've thought about it a lot," Alison said, tapping her fingernail on the tabletop. "The way I see it, there are two options. Either God created men and women absolutely equal—which is what I would like to believe—or he created them not at all equal, part of an inscrutable hierarchy, beyond anything we can understand today. Either way, things were messed up when Adam and Eve sinned."

"A hierarchy?"

"Well, I hate to think about it, but God could have created a hierarchy which included everything—the godhead, angels, men, women, right on down to the animals and plants. It's hard for us to imagine in today's society since we're so hung-up on equality, but in the beginning, who knows? It might have been different. Before man sinned, before the beings on the higher levels began lording it over the beings on the lower levels, it could have been a beautifully satisfying arrangement—everyone exactly where he belonged doing exactly what he was created to do—every relationship in perfect harmony. Just like in Ephesians, when it talks about the husband being head of the wife as Christ is head of the Church. And there are other verses talking about a hierarchy within the godhead itself."

She paused to sip her coffee. "In Luke, Jesus says, 'I confer on you a kingdom, just as my Father conferred one on me.' In John, Jesus talks about his dependency on the Father, and how we depend on him. It's kind of confusing, but it seems like the idea of a hierarchy is there, even within the godhead itself."

"But you don't like that idea," I said.

"Well, no. I'd rather think that God created us equal. I think that when the Bible talks about submission it is talking about mutual submission, not about God creating women subservient to men. The same chapter in Ephesians that talks about wives submitting to their husbands is really emphasizing mutual submission—submitting to one another for Christ's sake. And it goes on to talk about husbands loving their wives sacrificially, like Christ loves the Church." I nodded my head. "Anyway, if there are verses that suggest a hierarchy within the godhead, there are other verses emphasizing the equality and oneness of the godhead—a oneness I think God wants people to share. Before Jesus left the earth he prayed for that. 'Protect them by the power of your name,' he said, 'the name you gave me—so that they may be one as we are one.' "

"Where's that?" I said.

Alison waved her arm through the air. "Oh, I don't know, John sixteen or seventeen. But then," she said, leaning forward eagerly, "there's that wonderful verse in Philippians. 'Who, being in very nature God, did not consider equality with God something to be grasped.' In very nature God," Alison repeated, slapping her hand on the tabletop. She shook her head in wonder. "I don't know," she said. "It's almost as if any idea of a hierarchy within the godhead is really just a concession to sin—to the role Jesus played on earth in order to reconcile man to God—that it wasn't really in the very nature of things. If that's true, then it could be true of men and women too—that any idea of hierarchy is really just a concession to sin—not a picture of reality, of the nature of things."

Alison ran her fingers through her dark, wavy hair. "I don't know, I haven't figured that out yet. Anyway, after the Fall, men, because they were bigger and stronger, began to lord it over women." Her voice rose. "Then, in order to preserve their position of power, I think they began to formulate it into doctrines and religious tenets."

By this time Alison was practically pounding the table. "If man had remained innocent, like in the Garden, there wouldn't have been this antagonism between men and women. But once sin entered the picture, all was lost. It was each man—get that, Rebecca?—each man for himself. The survival of the fittest."

I stared at Alison. I wondered how the ladies in my Bible study group would have responded to this. I scratched my head. "Well, I still think that it's the man who is supposed to be the leader. When Paul writes to Timothy, he says that he doesn't let women teach men or lord it over them, because Adam was created first. I mean, there must be some sort of lesson there or Paul wouldn't have referred back to the creation story in the first place."

"Well, following that kind of logic, why not talk about how animals were created before man? If the order of creation is so important, why aren't the animals in charge?" Alison shook her head. "Some men will use anything to prove they're supposed to be boss."

I threw up my hands. "Oh, now you've gone too far." I shook my head. "You can't dismiss what's written in the Bible that easily."

"Well, maybe you can't," Alison said. "But I can. But I admit I haven't dismissed it easily. In fact, I haven't dismissed it at all—just put it on hold, put it on hold until I can begin to make some sense out of it."

I continued to shake my head. "I don't know, but, no. No." I was still shaking my head as I poured each of us a fresh cup of coffee. "Cream?" I asked. As always I was embarrassed I had to ask. I knew people who could remember for twenty years if someone took cream or sugar. I couldn't remember for twenty minutes. Alison shook her head. I poured a little cream in my own cup and sat back down.

"The real point is," Alison continued, waving her finger lightly through the air, "you don't really believe half the stuff you're spouting."

"I think I believe it," I said, feeling foolish as I heard my own words. I nodded my head. "I think I do."

Alison lifted her chin slightly and looked at me from under lowered eyelids. "And I think you don't. All I'm trying to say is, be honest with yourself."

I frowned. I couldn't figure out where Alison was coming from. I found her honesty and openness refreshing. But at the same time she made me feel uncomfortable. Her words were an echo of the thoughts I'd always been afraid to verbalize. Why was I scared to say out loud the things I was thinking? Was I afraid I'd be challenged? Or did I fear my doubts would prove correct and I would be left floating about with no anchor? Why did it all matter anyway? If Eliot was happy being my provider and protector, why should I mess with it? He didn't like it when I asserted myself. I was sure he loved me most when I tried to be sweet and submissive. I rested my elbows on the table and leaned toward Alison.

"Alison, it seems to me there are few things in life more important than being loved. If I started throwing my weight around and lost Eliot's love, what good would it do me? I'd have lost the most important thing in the world to me."

Alison looked straight into my eyes. She didn't smile. "Rebecca, if you are pretending to be something you are not, and if Eliot loves that person you are pretending to be, then he doesn't love you anyway. He loves a lie. Being yourself means risk. Eliot might reject you. On the other hand he might love you—you, the real you, for the first time. If you continue pretending to be something you're not, Eliot may go right on loving the shadow he thinks is you, but you will never feel loved. You see, Rebecca, Eliot may not know it's not the real you he's loving, but you will. You'll never feel really loved that way." Alison shook her head. "Ever."

CHAPTER
8

ALISON agreed to go to the Bible study with me. But she made me promise I wouldn't let her make a fool of herself.

"Don't let me get into any arguments," she said.

"OK," I promised.

We made it through the Bible study without disgracing ourselves, and in the following weeks we became good friends.

But her words rankled. In fact, they clattered and collided from side to side in my mind. Was I just pretending? Did I believe what I was saying? And what about Eliot? Did he love me? The real me? The questions echoed back and forth through my brain and when the answers clanged to the surface I hushed them with the muffle of anxiety.

The Christmas season was approaching and I was thrown into my usual ambivalence. I couldn't decide if I loved the holidays or hated them. This year they promised to be especially trying. Dad was much worse. The reason for the doctors' uneasy silence had become painfully obvious. They had discontinued chemotherapy, and by mid-December I was vacillating between the hope that he'd get better and the wish that he'd go quickly.

It also seemed like Eliot had his own ambiguous feelings about Christmas. This year we both seemed torn between wanting to celebrate the birth of Jesus and wanting to forget the whole thing. As Christmas Day approached, however, I began to feel something stirring within me. It could only be described as the Christmas spirit—the spirit of life in a world going dead. Eliot remained immune. He had never recovered from the detachment that had settled over him at the start of the school year. I was not sure if he was growing even more preoccupied, or if it was just more obvious during the holidays.

"What do you think we should get Matthew this year?" I asked one evening after the children were in bed.

"I don't know. I'll leave that up to you." He was sitting at his desk, writing, pondering, reading, and then writing again.

"What are you working on?"

"Hmm?"

"What are you doing? Correcting papers?"

"Huh? Oh, no. No, Sylvia wanted some history background for her ethics class."

"Ethics class?"

"Yup—it's called Elementary Ethics."

"Are you cross-disciplining that class too?"

"No. I just told her I'd do some research for her."

"Can't she do her own research?"

"Sure she can, but it's easier for me. I'm more familiar with the resource materials."

"Well, it seems to me she's taking advantage of you. It's her job."

"I don't mind. I kind of enjoy it."

WHEN I showed him the ornaments I'd bought for each of the children he nodded his head. When I held up the one I'd bought for us, a tiny carved wooden bed with two little heads peeking out above the covers, he only moved his head slightly. Then he spotted the price tag. "That kind of seems like a lot of money for a Christmas ornament."

I quoted my favorite line from a short-lived television comedy. "A gift for the soul is never extravagant," I said. I expected him to cower in the face of such sagacity. He merely shrugged.

"We'd better get our tree pretty soon," I said. "It's only a week and a half away."

"I'll get it Saturday." Pencil between teeth. Fingers running through hair—stroking thoughts into order.

"Saturday?" Keep voice sweet. "It will only be up for a week. Couldn't you pick one up some afternoon after school?"

"I won't have time until this weekend." Reading. Pondering. Gently tapping the pen against his teeth. A flourish of writing as a new thought presented itself.

ON Saturday when Eliot came home with the tree, I was appalled. Normally he took great pains in selecting our Christmas tree, as if his manhood were on the line—great white hunter come home with big tree. But when I saw the tree he selected this year, I was speechless. It was a Douglas fir—the skinniest Douglas fir I had ever seen. *Transparent* was the word that came to mind. On top of that, about a third of the way up it had a crook. The top two-thirds angled off to the side. I hoped the decorations would help, but I had my doubts. It has always seemed to me that the skinniness of some Christmas trees is only accentuated by the addition of ornaments. Skinny trees don't have enough branches to hide the light cord, and there's nothing as obscene as an exposed electrical cord.

Eliot chopped off a few inches at the bottom of the trunk. He shifted it around in the tree stand, trying to put the bottom in the stand at an angle so the top would be straight. But when he placed the tree in front of the large front window in the living room, there was no denying the fact that it was crooked. It was a crooked, skinny, ugly tree.

As soon as Eliot had strung the lights on the tree he disappeared into his den, muttering something about having papers to correct. I was irritated that he was leaving the decorating to me and the children. For some reason it made me feel deserted—like a forlorn woman with her runny-nosed children standing on a street corner, shivering in the cold.

Popcorn. Popcorn would fill the house with the warmth and aroma of a happy family. I popped some corn and dribbled melted butter over the top. The children walked back and forth from the tree to the pile of decorations, an ornament in one hand and a fistful of popcorn in the other. Kernels of buttery corn fell to the floor and were crushed into the carpet by stockinged feet as the children hooked one ornament after another onto the straggly branches.

The children were strangely quiet, so I put some Christmas records on the stereo to fill the silence. I lit the bayberry candle—the one I'd been saving for Christmas Eve—and it filled the air with its aroma. It blended with the smell of popcorn and the quiet strains of "Silent Night" that floated from the stereo.

They were all there—the sounds and smells of Christmas. But it didn't feel like Christmas. There was something missing. Inside of me. And Eliot wasn't there. And the tree was crooked. And the cord of the lights was exposed for all to see—an obscene reminder that none of it was magic.

What was Eliot doing? Why wasn't he helping us? All of a sudden it seemed so ugly. It was ugly and awful and I hated it. Wasn't he a part of this family anymore? I stood next to the tree holding the fragile glass ornament I'd bought for Eliot and me the year before. Suddenly I drew back my arm and threw the delicate ornament against the living room wall. The children stared at me in amazement and I burst into tears.

"Mom?" Shelly said. "Why did you do that?"

"I don't know. I don't know," I said, as tears streamed down my face. As I swept up the shattered pieces of glass I told the children I was sorry for losing control.

"Now just what did that accomplish?" I asked myself. "Nothing. Nothing at all. Throwing things doesn't solve a thing."

WE opened our gifts on Christmas Eve. The next day we drove out to the farm to spend Christmas with my parents. My sister Susan and her husband, Lance, had arrived at the folks' Christmas Eve and were staying through New Year's Day. I was glad. Mom would have help for a week, anyway.

Lance and Susan had barely gotten in on the last days of the flower children. When Susan had come home from college with long straight hair and flowers embroidered on her jeans, she had merely seemed in harmony with the times. But when she brought Lance home for a visit, the sight of them together created a different impression.

"They look like hippies," Eliot had said, straight as an arrow even as a young adult.

"Well, I don't think they're actually hippies," I had responded, shrugging my shoulders. "They're just casual."

And they weren't hippies. Not really. They had gotten married during their senior year at college, and after they graduated they had moved to Lincoln City, where Lance had opened a bookstore. "See?" I said to Eliot. "Would a hippie start a business?"

"You just wait and see," Eliot said, raising his eyebrows. "That store will look like a hippie hangout—probably smell like marijuana."

Their store did look rather like a hangout, but it didn't smell like marijuana. Over the years Eliot had come to respect Lance for his unswerving determination to do what he wanted, regardless of social pressure, and Lance respected Eliot.

ABOUT midmorning Lance walked into the kitchen, where I was peeling carrots for the relish tray. "Something the matter with Eliot?" he said.

Fear. "I don't think so. Why?"

"I don't know. He just acts funny. He's hardly said a word all morning."

It was true. Eliot had stopped briefly in the bedroom to speak to my father and then had plopped on the couch in the living room with his nose in a newspaper. He seemed oblivious to the children's restless movements, and equally unaware of the adult conversation going on around him. He stared at the newspaper with a faraway look in his eyes. I didn't think he was even reading it. Just staring. And smiling, kind of.

Our three children were moving about the house like panthers, the way they do when they're waiting for something good to happen. They're too excited to sit still, but are afraid if they make a wrong move their expected prizes will be snatched away. My own voice echoed inside my head, and I understood their anxiety. "If you kids don't settle down we're going to forget the whole thing," I'd said on various occasions and in diverse tones of voice over the years.

It was strange to eat Christmas dinner with Dad in the next room. Mom had to go in and feed him before the rest of us sat down to eat. It reminded me of when the kids were babies and I would hurriedly feed them before dinner and put them down for a nap, hoping they would go to sleep so I could eat an uninterrupted meal. Did Mom ever feel like letting him go hungry? He wouldn't have cried like the babies had. He probably wouldn't even have noticed. He had very little appetite left. But Mom cared for him religiously. Unfeigned devotion. I thought of all the little things I did for Eliot, the little things I did to win his approval. Compared to Mother's selfless rituals of service my little offerings seemed profane. Something was missing.

After we had eaten and cleaned up the kitchen, I went in to visit with Dad for a few minutes before he took his nap. As I entered the bedroom I paused in the doorway a moment and studied my father before he sensed my presence. How much longer? He was lying perfectly still, his eyes closed, his hands folded lightly across his abdomen. He looked so fragile and white, it seemed the heavy quilt that covered him might bruise his body. His eyes fluttered open and he turned his head. "Becky," he whispered, lifting his hand a few inches from the bed. I walked toward him and took his hand in mine. "Merry Christmas, Daddy," I said, kissing him lightly on the forehead. The skin that my lips touched was dry and wrinkly—half-dead.

Something was different. I studied his face for a moment. He looked more vulnerable, more helpless than I had ever seen him. When I realized what had changed, my eyes filled with tears.

"What happened to your mustache?" I said.

"Mom shaved it off."

How could she? Anger. Daddy had always had a mustache. Now everybody wore mustaches, but when I was a little girl my father was the only man I knew who had one. In my eyes it had lifted him above the plane of mortal men—made him a messiah almost. And me the daughter of a messiah.

I stared at my father's face, shorn of its immortality.

He was going to die.

For the first time I realized he was really going to die. I knelt beside the bed, pressed my face into the quilt, and sobbed.

"Becky, Becky," he said, running his fleshless fingers over my hair. "It's all right. It's all right."

I lifted my head. "Daddy, I love you," I said. And I couldn't remember the last time I'd told him that.

"I know," he said. He quit stroking my head. His bony fingers clamped themselves around a clump of my hair and he held on. I could feel the tension in his hand as he squeezed his fingers together, the tension causing his hand to tremble slightly. "I know," he repeated.

I wiped my face on the sleeve of my blouse and pulled a chair close to the bed. I sat down, taking my father's hand in mine. "What do you think about when you're lying here all day?" I asked.

"Oh, I don't know." His free hand fluttered across the top of the quilt, and he tugged at the strands of yarn that were tied into the quilt every eight inches or so. He pulled a partial strand of yarn loose and rolled it between his fingers until it formed a tiny ball, barely big enough to see. "I think about heaven. What it will be like." He turned his head toward me. "And I worry about Mom. How she'll get along when I'm gone." He turned his head away and his eyes looked far away, to a place I couldn't see.

"She'll do fine," I said. "She'll probably surprise all of us." She had begun to surprise me already. I suspected she would continue to rise to whatever the occasion demanded. No more. No less. Like the farm. She had completed the arrangements for the crops with Mr. Bellows and had negotiated a lease with him for the next year. She seemed almost to enjoy taking charge. And she had always seemed so helpless. *You better ask your father. I'll have to check with my husband. I don't know anything about that. Walter handles those things.*

I noticed Daddy was lying still, his eyes closed. "I'd better let you take your nap," I said. His eyes fluttered open. "Don't worry about Mom," I said. "She'll be OK. And we'll take care of her."

"I know you will, Becky. I know you will."

"Merry Christmas, Daddy."

"Merry Christmas, Becky. Uh . . . I didn't get my shopping done this year. Mom did it for me. But I told her what to get. I hope you like it."

"I'll like it," I said, brushing back his white hair. Each year my father gave Susan and me a small charm for the charm bracelets he'd given us when we started school. The year I learned to ride a bike it was a tiny bicycle with miniature handlebars that turned. The year Shelly was born it was a tiny baby shoe. There was a span of years when even my father seemed to sense nothing was happening to me. He had to turn to outside events. Apparently nothing of significance happened to me the year the astronauts landed on the moon. Daddy gave me a tiny spaceman. That was the year Lance and Susan got married. Susan got a miniature wedding cake.

As I reentered the living room I noticed that Lance had finally drawn Eliot out of his silence. They were standing in a corner engrossed in conversation—Eliot doing most of the talking. The children were already crawling around below the tree, sorting out the presents.

When Grandma gave the word, we all tore into our packages. There was the sound of ripping paper and excited exclamations from the children.

"A model, oh, awesome. That's cool!"

Eliot and Lance opened the packages containing their annual shirts and neckties. "Thanks, Mom," they said, sounding both pleased and disappointed. I knew how they felt. They longed for something else. Something magic.

I had saved my father's gift for last. Holding the tiny white box in my lap, I wondered what it would be this year. I glanced at Susan. She was ready to open hers, too. I slipped the bright ribbon off the box and lifted the tiny lid. Nestled inside on a bed of cotton was a tiny gold charm. I held it in the air, puzzled. It looked like a miniature castle, or palace. I glanced at Susan again. The charm she held up was identical. She too looked confused, and we turned to Mom.

"It's a mansion," she said without elaboration.

I furrowed my brow. Mansion. "Oh," I said. *In my Father's house are many mansions*. I held the tiny mansion by the clasp and let it dangle before my eyes. It was the last charm I would add to my bracelet. It glittered, and there were tiny reflections of the Christmas tree lights against its turrets and walls. *I go to prepare a place for you.* Susan was still staring at her charm in puzzlement. "In my Father's house are many mansions," I said.

"Oh," she said, smiling.

"That's where Grandpa's going, isn't it?" Tyler asked.

Sometimes he amazed me.

Suddenly Matthew's face brightened. "He's going to walk on streets of gold," he said, summing up his knowledge of heaven. "Can I see it, Mommy?" I put the miniature palace into his outstretched palm, which, even on Christmas Day, managed to look grimy.

"Look, Tyler," Matthew said. "This is where Grandpa will live." He pointed to the big tower at the center of the mansion. "This is where I'll live, and," he pointed to a tiny turret on the left side of the castle, "you can live here."

"Why do I have to live in the littlest one?"

"'Cause you're the littlest, dummy."

"Matthew, it's not nice to call anyone a dummy," I said.

"I'm tired of being the littlest. Mommy, will I still be littlest in heaven?"

"I don't know, Tyler," I said. "But I can tell you one thing. If you are, it won't matter." I paused. "I don't think it will matter."

After the presents were all opened and exclaimed over, Lance and Eliot gathered up the bright disarray of ribbon and Christmas wrap and gradually added it to the fire in the fireplace. It seemed strange to see Eliot and Lance poking the papers into the fire. That was Dad's job. He had always spent a good part of Christmas afternoon fussing with the fireplace and the wrapping paper—trying to decide if this or that ribbon was worth saving.

Mom brought out a cart loaded with oranges, nuts, candy, and Christmas cookies.

"Why can't I ever make divinity like this?" I complained. "Mine always crystallizes."

"Mine too," Susan chimed in.

"The weather has to be right," Mom said, "the right amount of moisture in the air."

Susan and I looked at each other and rolled our eyes to the ceiling. We didn't ask how much moisture was the right amount. We didn't want to know.

We spent the rest of the afternoon snacking, visiting, and trying to figure out how to play backgammon.

"Why don't you read the directions?" Matthew asked.

"Don't be fresh," Susan retorted.

A LITTLE after dusk I began gathering things together, starting a pile by the back door. "This is the Adamson pile," I announced.

When Lance asked if he could help, I handed him the keys to the trunk and followed him to the car with an armload of presents.

"I finally got him talking," Lance said, as we piled our paraphernalia into the trunk.

"Who? Oh, Eliot."

Lance nodded. "Once he got going he wouldn't stop. It sounds like he has a good chance of becoming department head next year—with Dr. Satter retiring."

I nodded my head, but didn't reply. I couldn't believe Eliot still hadn't even mentioned the possibility to me.

Lance continued. "He was also telling me about the classes he's been cross-disciplining. Philosophy?"

"Yes," I said. "He and Sylvia Weston have been team-teaching some of the history and philosophy classes."

"Oh, it's a woman. He didn't mention that. He couldn't think of the professor's name."

"He couldn't think—?" I stopped. Then I nodded my head slowly. "Sylvia," I said. "Sylvia Weston."

CHAPTER 9

JANUARY 20 was Eliot's birthday—his fortieth. It seemed a wonderful twist that Eliot, with his dusky nature, had been born in January, the bleakest month of the year. I liked to think he had been delivered during a storm, as high screeching winds assaulted brittle, creaking tree branches. I could imagine his first baby wail blending with the whine of the wind until they trailed together into an endless howl that reached back through the pages of history and shined forth from his eyes into the present.

A party seemed so inappropriate for the occasion, but this year I felt trapped. It was a tradition among our friends to throw a surprise party for the husband's fortieth birthday. It was a mystery to me how something could be both a tradition and a surprise, but as Eliot's birthday approached I began tossing around the possibilities in my mind.

I decided if I was going to give a surprise party for Eliot it was going to be, first of all, a genuine surprise, and second of all, grand. The more I thought about it, the more convinced I became that Eliot's birthday party could be the highlight of Milford's social year. I had to admit that since the college president's wife was assumed to be the queen of Milford's social life, and she habitually served Kool-Aid or Hawaiian Punch at her social events, it wouldn't be too hard to cause a stir in the college community.

I enlisted the help of Alison and Dave. We sent invitations to a hodgepodge of relatives, friends from church and work, and childhood cronies. Our plan had just the right mixture of intrigue, signals, and split-second timing to make it exciting. I felt sure that the chances of it misfiring were small, especially because Eliot still seemed so distracted.

Weeks before his birthday I began making canapes and putting them in the freezer. After freezing two or three elaborate canape trays, I worried that Eliot might come across them somehow, so I began storing them in the freezers of neighbors and friends. I got so carried away I feared when it came time to collect them for the party I wouldn't be able to remember where I had stashed them all. I made a list of the different hiding places but was afraid Eliot would come across it and wonder what it was. I tore it up and threw it away. I tore it into tiny pieces that fluttered and drifted slowly into the waste can like a miniature snowstorm.

I must have tried a dozen punch recipes. I was determined that no one, not even the most obtuse of our acquaintances, would ever accuse me of having served Hawaiian Punch.

If Eliot noticed we were having more punch around the house than usual he didn't say anything. Besides, Eliot was so preoccupied that sometimes I felt my careful plotting was a total farce. It seemed silly to worry about keeping a secret from a man who wouldn't have noticed if I'd started wearing a bone in my nose.

I spent the entire week before the party in a frenzy. I called Alison at least three times each day to make sure I hadn't forgotten anything. I called Marlene and repeated the signal I would give her, Tom, and the others when Eliot was taking his shower.

"Do you think he suspects anything?" I asked again and again. Then I would answer my own question. "I don't think he does. I'm just sure he doesn't suspect a thing."

"He doesn't suspect a thing," Alison would assure me each time.

When the big day arrived I was a nervous wreck. At breakfast I reminded Eliot twice that we were going out to dinner with Alison and Dave—that was part of the plan—and that he should try to get home from work on time.

"I'll try," he mumbled.

After he left the house I jumped in the car and raced from house to house collecting my trays of cookies and canapes—a reverse Santa Claus.

"Don't forget," I would cry as I drove off. "Be ready before 6:30."

ELIOT arrived home from work forty-five minutes early, and I was thrown into a fresh panic. What if he decided to take his shower right away? Tom and the others wouldn't be ready, and if Eliot got out of his shower before Tom and the others arrived the whole plan would be ruined.

"Oh, Eliot, you're home early," I said. My voice was high, like when I used to say my pieces at the Christmas program.

"Well, the way you kept after me this morning I thought I didn't dare be late." His voice was irritated.

"Oh, well, good. Good. I'm glad you're home."

Eliot started for the stairway. "Just a minute, Eliot, why don't you have some iced tea? You have plenty of time."

"I'm not thirsty."

"How about some crackers and cheese?"

"Crackers and cheese?"

I had never in our eighteen years of marriage offered him crackers and cheese after work.

"Yeah. Sure. I fixed up a tray of hors d'oeuvres to have with Alison and Dave before we leave for dinner."

"Nah, I'll wait till they get here. I think I'll go take my shower."

"There might not be any hot water. I just showered, did a load of laundry, and ran the dishwasher." I bit my lip. The shower and laundry would have been sufficient. The dishwasher was overkill. What if he went to the dishwasher for a glass and found it filled with dirty, unwashed dishes?

I glanced at the clock. It was 5:45. Tom and the others planned to be ready by 6:30. I had forty-five minutes to stall him. So far I had managed to keep him in the kitchen a total of three minutes. I was already out of ideas.

"Oh, Eliot," I said suddenly. "Matthew has been driving me crazy because the chain on his bicycle is broken. Do you suppose you could look at it before you get cleaned up?"

Eliot looked displeased and I was ready to tell him to forget it, but I knew I would only have to make up some other excuse. I pressed on. "Really, Eliot, he needs to ride his bike to school. I'm tired of taking him. It can't be anything too complicated."

Eliot sighed. "Oh, I suppose I can look at it." He headed for the garage.

I studied the set of his shoulders as he closed the door behind himself. Bad mood.

Once I had thrown myself into the preparations for Eliot's party, I hadn't really doubted its eventual success. I had been nervous and excited for weeks, but I hadn't really considered the possibility of a disaster. Now, for the first time, I was afraid I had made a terrible mistake. I imagined Eliot glumly munching an hors d'oeuvre while a whole houseful of guests tried to cheer him. I imagined the loud laughter and not funny jokes as everyone tried to convince everyone else they were having a wonderful time. I sank into the kitchen chair and buried my head in my arms.

I wanted to cry.

AT 6:25 I called Eliot in from the garage, telling him I thought he should take his shower. As soon as I heard him turn on the water I hurried to the back door and onto the sidewalk. I looked down the street to the corner of Church and Main where Tom and the others were supposed to be waiting.

"Oh, no," I muttered. "Where are they?"

The corner of Church and Main was deserted. I waited for a few minutes, then headed back toward the house. Just before I reached the porch I turned around and walked back to the curb again, craning my neck, trying to see some movement beneath the streetlamp. Finally I made out one figure and then several more. I waved my arm frantically, uncertain whether or not they could see me. Apparently they did, because they headed toward me, walking swiftly. Soon there was a whole sidewalk filled with people. I smiled in satisfaction and hurried into the house to make sure the water was still running in the shower.

It was.

I held the porch door open as the first guests came up the walk. I put my finger to my lips and said quietly, "He's in the shower." They tiptoed inside and I pointed them toward the kitchen where they were to hide until he got out of the shower and into his clothes. Just as the bulk of the group was streaming through the back porch, Eliot burst into, "When It's Springtime in the Rockies," his favorite shower song. I slapped my hand across my mouth to keep from laughing, and I had to quiet several others who were snickering too.

The shower stopped. I heard the scrape of the shower curtain along the rod as I shooed the last of the party guests into the kitchen. This was the trickiest part. Eliot had to get from the bathroom to our bedroom without realizing the kitchen was full of people. I held my hand in the air and a hush settled over the kitchen. I held my breath, fearing Eliot might come into the kitchen for a drink of water. Then I heard the creak of the stairway and I began to breath again.

While Eliot dressed I led the guests into the living room and they arranged themselves at the bottom of the stairway. I handed out party hats and horns. Then I ran up the stairs to see if Eliot was dressed.

"Are you about ready?" I asked. "Alison and Dave should be here any minute."

"I'm coming, I'm coming." Apparently his shower hadn't improved his disposition.

"I'll be waiting downstairs," I replied sweetly, hoping Eliot wouldn't say anything too obnoxious within earshot of the others.

WHEN Eliot came down the stairs he was surprised. He was really surprised.

"I don't believe this," he said again and again.

He walked to the bottom of the stairs and mingled among the guests, pumping the hands of his friends, some of whom he hadn't seen since high school. His eyes, a little bright, scanned the group again and again. I couldn't tell if he was amazed at all who were there, or if he was looking for someone who was missing.

Tom and Marlene had prepared a "This Is Your Life" skit, which was mildly funny in places and sloppily sentimental in others. Everyone endured it, hoping it would get better. It didn't. We went around the room and everyone told something funny about Eliot. I wanted to tell about the time he made love to me wearing his black socks, but I glanced at Eliot, and instead I told how he used to suck his thumb in the boys' lav.

After that, Eliot gave a short speech. Then I brought out the refreshments—tray after tray of canapes, cookies, meats, and cheeses. My punch was a roaring success. Alison held up her cup and said, "You did good." I laughed.

Dave, standing nearby, said to Eliot, "Hey, how come Sylvia's not here?"

I turned to Alison. "We invited her. Did you hear from her, Alison?"

"Yeah. I thought she was coming. I was sure she said she'd be here."

Eliot frowned slightly.

"That's funny," Dave said. "I wonder why she didn't come."

A few minutes later Eliot was telling a group of people about the fishing trip he'd taken in the fall. "You wouldn't believe all the salmon we caught," he said. "One was over thirty pounds." He paused. "I have some pictures. Give me a minute to find them. You won't believe the size of those things."

I was circling the room with a fresh pot of coffee when I overheard him and remembered I had cleaned out our bedroom closet and moved his photography equipment to the hall closet. Two guests were standing near me with empty coffee cups in their outstretched hands. I filled them and then asked Alison if she would mind taking the pot around the room. Alison, who always found the servant role difficult, reluctantly agreed.

I followed Eliot up the stairs.

When I got to the top of the stairs I had a clear view into our bedroom and was surprised to see Eliot by the telephone with his back to me. I heard the electronic beeping of the touch-tone phone as Eliot completed his call.

"Hi, Syl? This is me."

I stopped short. *Syl? Sylvia? Why would Eliot be calling Sylvia?* I slipped into the alcove just outside our bedroom door. The alcove was one of the reasons I'd fallen in love with the house. Eliot thought of it as wasted space. I had admitted it served no useful purpose, but I loved it. Now, I realized, it did have a function—it was a place to hide while eavesdropping. Eliot's voice was quiet, but I could make out his words clearly.

"Why didn't you tell me about this stupid party? . . . Well, I was surprised all right. But you know I don't like surprises. . . . " Eliot chuckled deep in his throat. "Well, that's different . . ." He chuckled again. "I think it might have looked better if you'd come. People are asking about you, wondering why you aren't here." I heard the squeak of the bed springs and knew that Eliot was sitting on the bed. Our bed. "I understand. I don't blame you. But I miss you. I just wish you were here . . . yeah, me too . . . I love you, too."

I couldn't hear anything after that. My ears were ringing, and although my eyes were closed, they were bruised by a blinding beacon of light. I was unable to move, immobilized and helpless like the deer my uncle used to spotlight in his orchard. While they were paralyzed by fear—their eyes wide and startled, their bodies frozen—he would raise his rifle. I had always carried in my mind the vision of those startled eyes, and the sound of their bodies thudding against the ground.

I was one of them, my only escape a frenzied dash down the stairs before Eliot saw me. Instead I sagged against the wall, unable to move.

When Eliot emerged from the bedroom he stopped short and stared at me. "I was looking for the pic—" Then his eyes met mine and he stopped. He was silent a moment, his face suddenly blanched. "How long have you been here?"

"Long enough," I said, although there was no sound, just the movement of my lips.

CHAPTER
10

THE only thing I remember about the rest of the party is that at one point Alison asked me about my tarts.

"Where are those tarts you were telling me about, Rebecca? Those little pecan ones that were supposed to be so good? Did your kids eat them?"

I stared at her blankly. Then I remembered. I had secreted them in my mother's freezer and had forgotten about them. "I don't know," I said.

AT LAST they were gone.

But as soon as the door closed behind Alison and Dave, who had lingered awhile to assure me the party had been a huge success, I wanted to call everyone back. All at once, being left alone with Eliot, having to talk about it, seemed like the worst thing in the world to me.

My right hand was still on the doorknob, and I leaned my back against the door.

I stared at Eliot.

"How long?" I asked.

Eliot took a deep breath. "Several months. Three months."

I slid my body along the wall until I reached the corner and then squeezed myself into it as if I needed the support of both walls. I shook my head from side to side. "Why, Eliot? Why?"

Eliot stared at me. The hint of pain in his eyes had changed to agony and he shook his head. "I don't know." He held out his hands and let them fall. "I'm sorry, Rebecca, but I can't tell you why. I don't understand myself." He raised his eyes to mine, and his brows were lifted slightly, his eyes wide and perplexed. "I couldn't even believe it myself half the time. I kept saying to myself, 'I can't be doing this. Why am I doing this?' But I was; I was."

"What now?"

"I'll break it off."

"I don't believe you."

"I swear Rebecca, I'll quit seeing her."

"It's not that easy. You'll see her at school every day. Besides, you love her. You said so. I heard you. You love her!" My voice had risen and I could hear the ragged edge of my own hysteria.

Eliot shook his head. "Not like I love you, Rebecca. Not like I love you. I'll work it out. I swear I will." He looked away—stared across the room at the blackness outside the window. "I'll work it out."

I pushed myself away from the wall and started up the stairs.

"Rebecca, please don't walk away from me. Let's talk."

I continued up the stairs and into our bedroom where I had left my purse. I opened it up, and as I came back down the stairs I riffled through it, looking for my car keys. My fingers touched them and they jingled slightly.

"Where are you going?" Eliot asked. He sounded like the kids used to sound when they heard the jingle of my car keys.

"I don't know."

"What do you mean you don't know? What do you think you're doing?"

"I don't know. I just have to get away and think."

"Rebecca—"

"Shut up, Eliot." My voice was barely audible. "Shut up." I squeezed my eyes together and closed my hands into fists. The keys pressed into my palm and I could feel the zigzag edges making indentations on my skin.

I turned and stepped out into the night. As I walked down the sidewalk I was aware that I was violating an agreement that had not been breached in the eighteen years of our marriage. In the early months of our marriage, Eliot and I had made a covenant—we had promised never to walk out on each other in the middle of an argument. We could throw things, scream, lock ourselves in the bathroom, or call names, but we would never, ever walk out. Ever.

Neither of us ever had.

I had spent three hours locked inside the bathroom one time, with Eliot standing outside begging me to please come out and talk things over. Another time Eliot had called me a stubborn jackass. We had, in fact, pushed the other options to the limits. But neither of us had ever walked out.

I was thinking about that as I walked toward the car. I felt guilty breaking our agreement. Breaking our vow. Broken vows. Forsaking all others.

I yanked the car door open and slid in behind the wheel, jamming the key into the ignition. As I backed away from the driveway, the tires squealed, and I could imagine Eliot coming out to examine the two black strips of rubber I left curving from the driveway to the street. I crammed the gearshift into forward and left two more black strips running straight toward Main Street.

ELIOT'S adultery might have been more bearable if I could have run away on a foggy night in New York City. In Milford, Oregon, it was not to be endured. In New York I could have stood on a foggy bridge—leaning over a gray span of slippery steel—contemplating suicide. But the Milford scenario was all wrong. There wasn't any bridge. There wasn't even any fog.

I drove through the main part of town and pulled into the parking lot of the Plaid Pantry. I didn't know what else to do. It was the only place in town open. I went inside and bought a pound of butter—and a Snickers candy bar. I don't even think I was low on butter.

Milford being what it was, I was in a dilemma over where to go once I'd left the Plaid Pantry. The town itself was L-shaped. Suddenly I was furious with Milford—angry at its stupidity. A town should have a core—a courthouse in the middle, something the town could center around.

"Stupid town," I muttered.

I drove up and down the streets of Milford, not knowing what to do or where to go. I thought about going to Alison's but I wasn't ready to talk—make explanations. I just wanted to go away—away from Milford, away from Eliot, away from myself. I tried to think things through, but my mind skittered and veered from the pain. I wanted nothingness. Just nothingness.

For eighteen years I had counted on Eliot, depended on him. No matter what ups and downs we had suffered, I had believed he was committed to me, believed that when the dust settled he would be there, committed to me, faithful. Like a rock. But little by little even rocks disintegrate. Grain by grain. Until all that's left is a heap of sand.

I should have felt the rock beneath my feet eroding piece by piece. I should have felt my feet slipping deeper and deeper into the sand. Icy waves had curled around my ankles and each one had pulled tiny grains of sand from beneath my toes, nibbling at my foundation, one tiny particle after another.

It wasn't until I heard the squeal of brakes that I noticed the stop sign. A white Buick screeched to a halt a few feet from me. We were stopped in the middle of the intersection staring at each other. The face of the other driver was contorted with rage. He shook his fist at me. "Oh, shut up!" I screamed. I slammed my car into reverse and backed out of his way. He shot across the intersection in an angry burst of smoke and squealing tires.

I cradled the steering wheel with my arms and let my head fall on them. I wanted to cry but couldn't. I was shaking, my entire body trembling with tiny shudders. I put the car into forward and started slowly down the street once again. What should I do? Where should I go? Why wouldn't my hands quit shaking?

I drove up and down the streets of Milford, but I knew I couldn't do that all night. When I passed a policeman for the third time, it seemed he slowed down. Had he noticed I was aimlessly drifting through Milford? I turned down the short end of the L and drove past the college. I turned around. The parking lot was behind a small grove of trees.

Not knowing where to go, what else to do, I drove into the parking lot and turned off the ignition.

As I sat in my car in the parking lot of Milford Junior College, I focused my attention on Building 4—the Humanities Building. Sylvia's building.

I was furious with Sylvia. I was enraged over Sylvia and her Humanities Building and her private office. I was incensed that she had long manicured fingernails and that she could make Eliot laugh, deep in his throat.

I was jealous that Sylvia could sneak Eliot away from me—that she could take something of mine and make it her own. But even as I examined my jealousy and hated it, I recognized that I had a right to be jealous. I didn't fight the anger. Even God was jealous when he saw his people turning away from him. *For the Lord your God is a consuming fire, a jealous God.*

But there was something else. More subtle. More evil. Snaking through my body, like a serpent in a garden was the insidious sin of personal envy. I wished I could be like Sylvia.

There was a tap on the window and a flash of light in my face. My hands flew to my face, a scream sticking in my throat.

It was the policeman. He motioned for me to roll down my window. I did, but my hands were shaking so badly it took me longer than usual.

"Are you all right, lady?" he said, shining his flashlight throughout the interior of the car.

"Yes," I said.

"You have some place to go? This is no place for a woman alone. Not at this time of night. You have some place to go?"

"Y-yes," I said. "I have a place to go."

I went home.

CHAPTER 11

WHEN people wanted to know why I suddenly decided to visit Susan in Lincoln City, I brushed their questions aside.

"Oh, I just haven't seen her for awhile," I said with a flip of my wrist.

But I couldn't leave town without running out to the folks.

Dad was very bad.

When Mother opened the door I was startled to see how tired she looked. How much longer could she take this—waking up each morning wondering if there was a corpse in the next bed? Would she know? Or would she just wake up and find it there? A body with no one inside.

As had become my custom, I fixed myself a cup of coffee before going in to see Daddy. I removed the little jar of Maxwell House Instant Coffee from the lower shelf and marveled at its smallness.

When I sat at the table, Mother was wringing her hands. "He's in so much pain," she said. "They want to put him in the hospital."

"Maybe that would be best."

"Oh, Rebecca, no. It would kill him." The irony of her words slipped past her. "He wants to be here, on the farm, with the quiet of the fields and the smell of the soil around him."

I nodded my head. "Can they do anything about the pain?"

"The nurse is going to teach me how to give him shots. Morphine, I think."

I stared at Mother. She had sensitive lips, and her eyes were so timorous they jumped at the least noise or sudden movement. I tried to imagine her poking a needle into Daddy's aching flesh.

"When?"

"Tuesday. I'm taking him in to the doctor again on Tuesday."

As I walked into the bedroom I realized it was the only room in the house that didn't smell like Ivory soap. Not any more.

I could make out Daddy's wiry frame under the thin blanket. His birdlike hands fluttered across the top, picking at the lint.

"How are you feeling?" I said. As always, I chided myself. *Stupid question. Stupid.*

Without moving his head he rolled his eyes upward so he could see me better. *Too weak to move? Too painful?*

"OK," he whispered.

I sat in the chair next to his bed. "I'm going to Susan's for a few days," I said.

"What?"

"Susan's. I'm going to Susan's."

"Oh. Susan's here?"

"No, no, Daddy. I'm going there." I pointed to myself and then swept my arms westward, trying to get him to understand.

"Oh." He nodded. He understood. "You like Susan?" he asked.

"Yes, Daddy. I like her very much."

"That's good. You used to fight a lot." He became agitated, moving his hands aimlessly.

I touched him on the shoulder. "I know. All kids do. We're all over that. We're good friends now."

"Good. Always wanted you to like each other."

"We do."

The small white bird hands quit fluttering. One bony hand settled on top of the other. I leaned forward, my hand on his shoulder, and kissed him on the forehead. I could feel the bones of his shoulder beneath the parchment layer of skin and I shrank inside. I imagined I could crush his feeble framework to dust if I pressed my fingers together.

"What about you and mother?" I said.

"What?" he said. He peered at me with his hollow eyes.

"Did you used to fight?"

He waved his skeleton hand through the air and smiled. "Oh, yes," he said. "We used to fight all the time. We argued about who was going to die first. We both wanted to be first. Didn't want to be left alone." His hands were trembling, but his eyes were alive. "We were young," he croaked. "Thought we were telling each other how much we loved each other." He shook his head. "Stupid kids. Didn't know a thing about love—just being selfish."

I did't say anything.

Daddy looked at me with solemn penetrating eyes and took my hand between his shaking fingers. "Going to Susan's, huh?"

I nodded my head.

His hands were quivering. He was tired from his long speech. "That . . . that wasn't the kind of fighting you meant . . . was it?"

I shook my head.

"We did the other kind too, Becky—the ugly kind." He patted my hand. "But it's not the fighting that's important."

"It isn't?"

He shook his head and pierced me with his wise old eyes. "It's the forgiving," he said. He gently wagged his skinny finger. "That's what really matters."

I nodded my head slowly. My throat felt raw.

WHEN I stepped back into the kitchen, Mother said, "Did I hear you say you're going to Susan's?"

"Uh-huh." I was fighting back tears.

"Why, whatever for?"

I flipped my wrist halfheartedly. "Oh, I just haven't seen her for awhile."

"Hmm. Oh, Rebecca, the funniest thing. You'll never guess what I found in the freezer yesterday."

"What?"

"Those pecan tarts. The ones you made for Eliot's party, remember? You forgot to come get them."

I stared at Mother. Then I pulled a Kleenex from the box on the counter and blew my nose. I turned away from her and mumbled something about having plenty of food at the party. "It went fine," I said. "We had lots to eat."

THAT evening Eliot paced back and forth across the kitchen begging me not to leave.

"Please, Rebecca, let's talk this out. Don't leave, don't run away."

"I'm not running away. I just have to have time to think. I can't think with you around."

"But we can't work things out if we're not even together."

I turned on him and I could feel the fire in my eyes. "Eliot, don't you dare stand there like a self-righteous prig and tell me what to do," I said, putting my hands on my hips. "You are in no position to be telling me what to do." Tears were coursing down my cheeks by then and my voice had risen an octave. "I have to think!"

"Rebecca, please," Eliot said, trying to put his arm around my shoulders.

I pushed him away. "Don't touch me. Don't you dare touch me."

THE turn-off to Susan's was just before the road dropped over one last hill into Lincoln City and a view of the Pacific Ocean. As I turned from the main highway onto the narrow road that wound its way around Delake, I was reminded of how effortlessly Susan and Lance had acquired the things they wanted. Shortly after they graduated from college Lance had received a small inheritance—just enough to start his own bookstore. A year later they had bought the house on the lake. The owner had died and the children were eager to sell. It was an older home, one of the few around the lake suitable for year-round living. It was red with white trim and large enough to be comfortable without looking pretentious. There was a large screened-in porch along the back. It had a boathouse at the edge of the lake and an acre of grass and trees.

The gravel crunched under the wheels of the station wagon as I pulled into Susan's driveway. Susan opened the front door as I approached the porch steps, suitcase in hand. There was a huge geranium in a pot on the porch, and I almost knocked it over with my luggage.

"Oh, be careful," Susan said. "That's my pride and joy."

"It is beautiful," I said. "How do you get it to bloom like that, in January?"

"I meant the pot," Susan said, "not the geranium. Alec made it for me."

"Alec?"

"My pottery teacher."

"Oh."

"How are you?" Susan asked, eyeing me closer than I liked.

"Fine," I said, but I felt like I was going to cry.

"Are you all right? What's wrong?"

I opened my mouth and almost blurted out that Eliot was having an affair, that's what was wrong, but then I closed my lips and shook my head. "I'm just tired, I guess. I didn't have any breakfast, just a doughnut and coffee." I had not explained to Susan why I was coming or how long I planned to stay.

"Come on, I'll fix you some soup," Susan said, taking me by the arm. "Leave your bag there. Lance can take care of it when he gets home."

Susan had a big pot of homemade vegetable soup bubbling on the stove. The steam from the soup mingled with the already moist air. There was the faintest aroma of mildew in their home—the smell that characterized all dwellings that close to the ocean. The sea-filled air covered everything with a gentle canopy of moisture, and I imagined I could even taste the salt against my lips.

"You aren't going to make me eat alone, are you?" I said.

"No. I've already had a bowl, but I'll have another."

"I don't blame you. It smells delicious."

"Mom's recipe."

"I might have known."

Susan sat very still for a moment. "How's Dad?" she said at last.

I shook my head. "He can't last much longer. Every time the phone rings I think,'This must be it.' I can't believe he's hung on as long as he has. He's just skin and bones."

Susan's eyes filled with tears. "Why can't he just go? Why can't he just get it over with?"

"How do you think Mom will handle it?" I asked.

Susan walked to the counter for Kleenex and dried her eyes. "I don't know. She'll cope I guess. What else can she do? Some things just have to be endured."

I stared out Susan's kitchen window and across the lake with its umbrella of fog.

"You're right, I guess," I said.

Susan patted me on the shoulder. "She'll get through it somehow."

"What if she doesn't?"

"She will."

THE next day Susan and I did some shopping in the little shops that lined themselves along the stretch of highway called Lincoln City. Lincoln City was actually four or five towns strung together under one name. They used to have names of their own—Nelscot, Delake, Taft—and I could never get used to considering that stretch of highway a town. Did calling them all by one name make it so? A funny thing about names. He had a funny thing about names. *Becca, Becca. OK, Becca?*

Susan and I went for a walk on the beach, and Susan acted like any minute she expected me to tell her why I was there. In fact, as we walked along the beach, I expected myself to tell her. But every time I opened my mouth to speak I just couldn't. It was too awful. I couldn't get myself to say the words. *Affair. Adultery.* There was no nice way to put it. It all hurt too much.

Susan had an appointment for lunch on Wednesday, so Lance invited me to go to the store with him. We spent the morning restocking the shelves. At noon his part-time clerk came in and Lance announced we were going on a picnic.

"I'll run to the deli and pick up our lunch," he said. "I'll be back in a flash." He was true to his word, and after he had given a smattering of instructions to the clerk, who had a bad memory, we walked the short distance to the beach. We took off our shoes and wended our way between the driftwood across the sand.

"There's a sheltered spot about fifty feet ahead," Lance said, pointing to a pile of logs providing a break from the wind. We scooted in behind the logs and Lance pulled out our lunch, ripping open the sack and spreading it flat. "A piece of cake, a pat of butter, and a bottle of wine," he said, "just like Little Red Riding Hood."

"Little Red Riding Hood had wine in her basket?"

"Sure, didn't you know that?"

"Not in my book she didn't. She had little tea cakes or something."

"Oh," Lance said with disdain. "You had the revised edition. I suppose the woodsman got there before the wolf ate Little Red Riding Hood, too."

"Well, yes. Ate Little Red Riding Hood? That's crazy! The woodsman saved her just in time."

"No, no. The woodsman had to cut open the wolf to rescue Little Red Riding Hood and her grandmother."

"Cut him open? That's barbaric."

"Well," Lance said, shrugging his shoulders, "that's the authorized version."

I shook my head.

It was one of those days when clouds occasionally drift across the sun to block out its warmth. There was enough bite in the air to make us shiver with cold and pull our coat collars close to our necks when the sun went behind a cloud. But when it forced its way out again its warmth was so delicious we didn't resent its absence, only reveled in the pleasure of its return.

Lance opened the bottle of wine and poured some into a styrofoam cup for me. I stared at the cup of wine in my hand. "I don't usually drink, you know."

"I know."

"Well . . . what?" I lifted the cup in the air with a gesture that asked him to explain himself.

"I thought you needed it," he said.

I looked into his eyes and he leaned forward, resting his elbows on his knees. "What's wrong, Rebecca? Why are you here?"

"What do you mean?"

"Come on. It's the middle of the school year. You've never come over here like this before. Something's wrong. What is it?"

"You're right," I said. "I think I do need this." I took a gulp.

"Take it easy," Lance laughed. "I don't want to have to carry you home." I licked my lips and took another swallow. "You're not going to tell me?"

I looked at him for a moment, blinking back quick tears. I shook my head again.

"By the way, Susan never did say where she was going for lunch. Was she meeting a friend?"

Lance broke off a piece of bread and a hunk of cheese and handed it to me. "She's having lunch with Alec."

I looked up. "Alec?"

"Her pottery teacher. She just might get serious about this pottery thing. Alec would like her to help him with some of his classes—become his assistant. I suppose that's what they're talking about today . . . maybe not . . . they have lunch together once in awhile just because—" He flipped his hand through the air. "Well, just because they want to."

I stared into my wine and twirled the cup in tiny circles, watching the rich red liquid form a miniature whirlpool. "You don't mind?"

Lance gazed across the ocean. His eyes watched one wave after another pound to shore. When he spoke his voice sounded perplexed. "I don't know. I don't know if I mind or not." He looked at me. "Most of the time I feel very comfortable with their friendship—Susan's been very open about it—but every once in awhile I think, Lance Marshall, you are an idiot." He shook his head. "I hate it when I feel like that—it's miserable."

I nodded my head, and for a moment we were both silent. "But isn't there a place for jealousy?" I said. "I mean, if your marriage is threatened, don't you have a right to be jealous?"

"Well, I suppose so . . . if your marriage is really threatened. I don't think mine is."

I rested my chin in my hands and watched a seagull dive into the ocean for something. The gull came back up, and I couldn't tell if it got what it was after. I looked into Lance's eyes. "But how do you know when to trust and when to be jealous? I mean . . . can't you go on trusting and trusting until it's too late?"

"What do you mean too late?"

"Well, I mean . . . too late. Too late to do anything about it."

Lance's eyes were gentle, but they locked mine in their grip and I could not turn away. "Exactly what good does being jealous do? Do you really think going through the misery of jealousy will stop anything from happening?"

I studied the minute grains of sand that had sneaked their way into the little openings on the rough bark of a nearby log. I shook my head. "No, I suppose not, but . . . " I hit my fist three times on the log. "It just seems like you ought to be able to do something."

Lance studied my face, and I read in his eyes an unasked question. I looked away. "I think I'd like some more wine," I said.

AFTER we'd finished our lunch we returned to the store and worked through the afternoon. We were down to the last box and both of us were tired. "Just a few more," Lance said. I was at the top of the ladder and he gave me a handful of books. I took them without looking at the titles. "Eliot," Lance said.

"Eliot?"

My voice was so strange and quiet, Lance turned around and stared at me. "Eliot," he repeated. "T. S. Eliot."

I looked at the books, but my eyes had filled with tears and I couldn't see the author's name. "One *l* or two?" I said. My voice was barely more than a whisper.

"One, just like your Eliot."

I turned my face away and nodded my head slowly. Finally I turned back to Lance. He could see I was crying.

"Rebecca," he said, searching my eyes, "what is it?"

"Eliot—," I began, but I couldn't continue. I lowered my head again and my shoulders began to shake.

Lance took my arm and helped me down from the ladder. "Come on, let's go home. I can finish this up tomorrow."

I NEVER did tell them. I knew I needed to talk to somebody but I just couldn't. After the incident in the bookstore with Lance, I knew that if I couldn't tell him then, with tears already streaming down my face, I never would. And after that things were a little awkward. Susan and Lance knew something was wrong but felt helpless to do anything since I wouldn't talk about it. Eliot called Thursday evening. Susan and Lance discreetly left the room, each finding his own excuse. Eliot begged me to come home. Since things were getting uncomfortable where I was, and since I didn't know what else to do, I agreed to come home the next day, in the late afternoon.

I had trouble sleeping that night, and the next morning I rose early, before Lance and Susan. The sky was cloudless, and as I looked out the window at the lake it was like a shimmering sheet of silver glass. I put on my robe and quietly let myself out the back door.

I was barefoot and the grass was still wet with dew. It was cold beneath my feet and against my legs. Some places it was as tall as my knees and I gathered my robe up to keep it from getting soggy and damp. It felt wonderful, all of it—the wet grass, the sun warm against my cheeks, and the feeling of being alone in the early morning world of shimmering sun and water.

I made my way through the grass to the boat dock and then walked across the teetering dock to the very end. The water went *sloop, sloop*, against the dock as it tipped back and forth with each of my steps. I sat on the end of the boat ramp and let my legs dangle over the side. My toes could barely touch the icy water, and I shifted so I could lower one foot in ankle deep. I swished it back and forth till it grew numb, then I let it hang still and soundless in the water. I leaned back against a pylon and pulled my robe above my knees, adjusting the belt so my robe wouldn't fall open. I leaned back and closed my eyes.

I was tired. I hadn't slept well. In the middle of the night I had climbed from bed and sat in front of the window staring at the lake. I had pressed my face against the cold damp windowpane and whispered, "Oh, Eliot, it hurts so bad." I wanted to tell him. I wanted to tell him how bad I hurt and how awful it was to feel betrayed. I wanted to cling to him and sob until some of the hurt had washed away. I wanted to look into his sorrow-filled eyes and hear him tell me he was sorry and that he loved me and that everything would be all right. I wanted to abandon myself to him and say, "Oh, Eliot, just love me, just love me."

But I felt the coldness of the windowpane against my cheek and moved my face away from the glass. My cheek was wet, a combination of tears and condensation. I touched my hand to my face and held it there. Then I leaned forward and pressed my face against the glass again, staring at the black, cold water of Delake. Devil's Lake, that was its name really. Delake was a euphemism. Dark and mysterious, like Eliot's eyes. What was entombed in those eyes? Did Sylvia know? Had she been able to plumb their depths? Had Eliot shared himself with her in a way he never could with me?

I hunched my back, pressed my forehead against my knees, wrapped my arms around my head, and sobbed. How could he? How could he share himself with someone else? I would never tell him how much he'd hurt me. I wouldn't even try to explain to him the agony of a person betrayed—the pain and alienation. Instead I would separate myself from him. But I would never let myself forget all the pain he'd caused. I would remember and I would make sure he knew I was remembering.

The lake was black and the encircling hills were silhouetted against the night sky. Lights burned in a few of the houses that zigzagged around the lake. They contrasted with the barrenness of the hills beyond.

Forgive and you shall be forgiven. Well, I just couldn't forgive. I couldn't; I wouldn't. He didn't deserve to be forgiven. I couldn't dig a hole deep enough to keep the hurt and anger from clawing its way back to the surface. And I didn't have the courage to try. I didn't want to dig and dig. I didn't want to waste my energy shoveling layer over layer—trying to bury something that wouldn't stay buried.

After crawling back into bed, shaking with cold, I tossed and turned restlessly, thrashing around in the bed with its slight aroma of mildew, nurturing a growing certainty that I would have to learn to take care of myself. Somehow during the long night I managed to separate myself from Eliot. I was no longer afraid to feel alone. Being alone was good. Being alone was strong and safe and good.

CHAPTER
12

I ARRIVED home late Friday evening. The kids were in bed and Eliot was on the couch watching television.

At least he was home—he wasn't with Sylvia.

Ten points for him.

When he saw me, he jumped up from the couch and rushed across the room. I thought he was going to hug me, but then he drew back. I was relieved. Maybe he sensed that.

"How are you?" he said.

"OK."

"How are Lance and Susan?"

"Fine."

"Good."

I looked around the room. "The kids are in bed?"

"Yes."

"How have they been? I missed them."

"Fine. We got along OK." He hesitated, then he reached toward me. "Rebecca—"

"Eliot, don't."

I lifted my suitcase and started up the stairway. Eliot followed me. When I got to our bedroom I set my suitcase on the floor and stood next to the bed, my hands at my sides.

Eliot sat on the bed and patted his hand on the spot next to him. I sat beside him, but I folded my hands in my lap and stared straight ahead. Eliot leaned forward, his hands clasped between his knees. He also stared straight ahead, and as his fingers worked against each other, his knuckles turned from red to white to red.

"I've broken off with Sylvia." He blurted the words out awkwardly. I couldn't tell if it was because he couldn't hold them back or because they were so difficult to say.

"I don't believe you."

"I don't blame you. But I'm telling you the truth."

I stared at him, stony-faced.

"I'm going to make it up to you, Rebecca. I'll make it up to you if it takes me the rest of my life."

I looked into his aching eyes and was surprised that I felt no response to the pain I saw. I shook my head. "You can never make it up to me, Eliot. We had something. It was ours, just ours. You took what was ours—you took that and shared it with Sylvia." I shook my head from side to side. "There's no way to make that up to me."

"But Rebecca, you're not even giving me a chance. Give me a chance. Let me try." I looked away and didn't reply. "Well, what—what are you going to do?" he asked.

"Nothing."

"Nothing? What do you mean nothing?"

"Nothing. I just mean nothing."

I turned to face Eliot and his face swam before me like a mirage. I could live with a mirage. Mirages were only a disappointment if you expected something good from them—an oasis of fresh flowing water in the midst of burning sand. But I expected nothing good from Eliot. He was a bad mirage, not a good one. And if a good mirage could not provide refreshment, then a bad mirage could not produce pain.

I leaned back a little and folded my arms. I looked directly into Eliot's face. My voice was controlled and even as I spoke. "Eliot, what I really ought to do is ask you to leave. But I can't do that." I shook my head. "I can't do that to the children. . . . I just can't do it. But," I said, shaking my head again, "if I ever find out you're seeing Sylvia, I swear I will. I'll kick you right out of this house." I could feel myself losing control and I stopped.

"I told you, I broke off with her. I won't be seeing her." He stared at me. "But what about us?"

I shook my head.

"What are you saying?" Eliot's voice was rising. "We're just going to live here together—side by side—like zombies? What kind of a marriage is that?"

I turned on Eliot in fury. "Don't you dare talk to me about what kind of marriage that is. Don't you talk to me about marriage at all. This is your doing, Eliot Adamson. You should have thought about what kind of marriage you wanted before you took the one we had and ripped the guts out of it." I clenched my fists and held my arms straight at my sides while my whole body shook. I longed for the release of tears—or something—some kind of release, but there was nothing—just choking anger and frustration.

We never talked about it after that. Sometimes I tormented myself by wondering how discreet Eliot and Sylvia had been. Did others know? Was it the talk of the campus? Sometimes I tried to imagine what their relationship had been like. How had it started? What did they talk about? How had it ended? If I caught Eliot staring into space I wondered if he was thinking about her. Did he miss her? Had they yelled at each other in the end? Had Sylvia pouted? Had they clung to each other as they said good-bye? I couldn't stand to think about it for long, but I hoped they had yelled. I hoped Sylvia had screamed at him, called him ugly names, made a fool of herself—her face contorted with rage. But I doubted it. I couldn't imagine Sylvia making a fool of herself. Sylvia was, above all, civilized.

Several weeks passed. Eliot and I had declared our home a noncombat zone. The smell of battle hung in the air, but no one wanted to fire the first shot. There were minor skirmishes, but neither of us wanted to start something we couldn't finish. When we spoke to one another it was guardedly, and we were careful to steer clear of controversial subjects—or personal subjects, or funny subjects, or interesting subjects.

As usual, February had tricked me into thinking spring had arrived. The days were often sunny, and I could make out little shoots on the tree branches as they came to life. When March arrived, the illusion continued.

The last morning of spring vacation Eliot announced he was going motorcycling.

I slammed the cupboard door.

"What's the matter with you?"

"Nothing."

"What do you mean, nothing? That door didn't slam shut by itself. What's the matter?"

"You never get around to doing things."

"What things?"

"Well, the bathroom, for instance."

Eliot sighed. "Rebecca, must you bring that up? I'll start the bathroom as soon as school is out."

"That's what you said last year."

"Well, last year was different."

"Last year was different all right."

Eliot's jaw moved to one side. "Rebecca, don't. I don't want to go round and round about the bathroom. Why don't you start a notebook or something—pick out some wallpaper—anything, just get some ideas together so when school is out we'll know where we're headed. That would be a good project for you."

That would be a good project for you. I could hear myself saying the same thing to Tyler when he was making a pest of himself. "Here, Tyler, why don't you go through these magazines and cut out all the pictures of puppies. That would be a nice little project for you."

Just after Eliot left, Marlene dropped by. It was a sunshiny day, and when I opened the door to let her in the birds were chirping so loudly I had to laugh. "They're going crazy," I said, looking up into the trees to see if I could spot them.

"They're building a nest—look." A bird flew into the maple tree, disappearing among the tender leaves. "Incredible, isn't it, that nesting instinct? I have a lot of it myself," Marlene said.

I had to agree. If there was one thing Marlene had, it was the nesting instinct. "Why don't we sit outside," I said. "How does iced tea sound?"

"Great."

I got the lawn chairs out of the garage, and we settled beneath the maple tree with our iced tea.

"I've been meaning to ask you," Marlene said. "How does it feel to be married to the head of the history department?"

I shrugged my shoulders. In February Eliot had been named head of the department. As far as I could tell, being married to Eliot the department head was no different than being married to Eliot the professor. Right now neither one was too exciting.

"It's no different."

After a few minutes we moved our chairs into the sun. It was too chilly in the shade.

"Did Eliot get any work done on the bathroom over spring vacation?"

I looked into my glass of tea, studying the shape of the ice cubes. Interesting things, ice cubes. "No," I said.

"You're kidding!" Her voice showed disgust, and she was eyeing me closely. "Don't you get impatient with him?"

I lifted my chin slightly. "I'm sure he'll start working on it as soon as school gets out."

"Well, I hope so," Marlene said, rising from her chair. "He's bound to get around to it sooner or later, I suppose." I started to get up. "Stay where you are," she said. "I have to run along. I'll put my glass on the back porch. Sit in the sun for awhile. It's good for you. You know, vitamin D . . . or is it A?" She waved her hand through the air. "Well, whatever. See ya."

"Bye."

I did sit in the sun for awhile. But not because it was good for me. I was too lazy to move. I glanced around the yard. The flower beds needed to be weeded already. Why did the weeds wake up before the flowers? And the grass needed mowing. It hadn't been mowed since last fall—just early enough in the fall to grow shaggy again and look disheveled all winter. Well, that was Eliot's job—the grass. If he wasn't always off riding that stupid motorcycle.

Was he? What if he wasn't? What if he was with Sylvia? No. I believed him. I believed him when he said he would no longer see her. I knew he didn't want to lose me. I knew our marriage was important to him. And it was important to me. The form was important—the family, the home, the social convenience. I hadn't realized that before—how important the outer shell of marriage was. Even though the insides were ripped out, I was clinging to the shell, like Faulkner's Miss Emily, who had slept with the corpse of her lover for ten years. And the insides had been ripped out, hadn't they? What was left if exclusiveness and fidelity were taken out of marriage? Was there something left? I thought I glimpsed something for an instant, but it slipped away before I knew what it was.

I closed my eyes and reminded myself that I had been betrayed. The word itself was weighty—worthy of being remembered.

I heard the telephone ring and waited for one of the children to answer it. Once. Twice. Answer the phone. Three times. Where were they? Four. Rats. I jumped from my chair and dashed across the yard to the back steps. Up the stairs. Into the kitchen. Out of breath. "Hello?"

It was mother. Daddy was dead.

CHAPTER 13

WE buried Daddy on Tuesday, a bright, sunny morning in late March—a morning when Dad would have been out on his tractor plowing his fields, not lying still and cold beneath the soil he loved.

I was not prepared for the finality of it. We all thought we were ready for him to die. He had lingered long and he wanted to go. But after Mother's call, when I had rushed out to the farm and had seen Daddy's still form beneath the thin blanket, without even the usual fluttering of his bony hands or the turn of his head as I entered the room, I was overwhelmed by the difference between life and death. For months I had thought of him as half-dead. But there is no such thing as half-dead. There is dead. And there is alive. And now he was dead. Full dead.

After the funeral there was a dinner at the church for all the relatives. Later in the afternoon most of the relatives gathered together once again at the farm. Everyone watched Mother, to see how she was holding up. She seemed to be doing well. Susan planned to stay on till the end of the week. That would help.

While I was rinsing out dirty coffee cups, I looked out the window over the sink and noticed Lance and Eliot visiting in the driveway, leaning on my uncle's new car. From time to time I saw them point to the tires, or inspect the grill. They were talking cars, a safe subject. I knew there was an awkwardness between them. I had never told Eliot anything about my stay with Lance and Susan. He didn't know whether or not I'd confided in them. Fine. Let him squirm.

When they came into the kitchen a few minutes later, I glanced in their direction. They both looked at me as if crying for help. I turned back to the sink and swished the dishcloth around and around inside a coffee mug. Let them figure it out.

When Susan came into the kitchen with another tray of dirty dishes, I leaned against the counter and brushed the hair from my face with the back of my hand. "I can't believe it," I said. "There is a never-ending stream of dirty dishes."

"Let me take over for awhile," Susan said. "You look bushed."

I handed her the washcloth. "Is Mom OK?" I asked.

Susan nodded her head. "She wondered if you could come out Thursday and help sort through Daddy's things."

"Thursday? Sure. I think so. What time?"

"I don't know. I suppose as soon as you get the kids off to school."

"That should work out fine." I nodded my head. "That way I can get some things done around the house tomorrow. The place has been in a state ever since Mother called."

Susan nodded her head.

WHEN I arrived at the farm Thursday morning, Susan and Mother were sitting at the kitchen table, having a second cup of coffee. They were still in their robes, their hair uncombed, their eyes a little puffy. I felt crisp and efficient when I walked in fully dressed, smelling like the out-of-doors. I imagined that was how Eliot felt each morning when he left for work—fresh and dressed and smelling of Aramis, while I sat at the table in my robe and slippers, barely awake.

"Have a cup of coffee, Rebecca," Mother said.

I sat down and she brought me a cup of coffee along with a stack of sympathy cards. I sorted through them slowly. *In Deepest Sympathy*. *In Times of Sorrow*. "This is a nice one from Mr. Bellows. Oh, here's one from Alison and Dave. That was sweet. They sent me one too.

You've met them, haven't you? He works with Eliot." Mother nodded her head, but I could tell she couldn't recall meeting them.

We sat at the table for a few minutes sipping our coffee, nobody talking. Finally Susan said, "Well, Mom, I suppose we should get dressed and dig in."

"I suppose so," she said.

"I'll straighten the kitchen while you two get cleaned up," I said. I was still feeling efficient.

WE stood in the middle of the bedroom and stared around us. Where to begin? "Shall we do the clothes first?" I said.

Mom sighed. "I suppose so."

We sorted through Daddy's clothes, trying to decide what to give to Goodwill and what to throw away. There really wasn't much worth saving. Dad had never been too concerned about his apparel. Sorting through the clothes was hard for Mother, but I was all right until we got to his bureau drawer, the one where he kept all the little odds and ends he'd saved over the years. There was a Father's Day card I'd made for him when I was in kindergarten. *To Daddy, I lov yu!* We put the drawer on the bed and sorted through the trivia while a lifetime of memories washed over the three of us. Way in the back of the drawer was a tiny box, the kind you get at jewelry stores.

"I wonder what this is," I said. I picked up the box and lifted the tiny lid. "What? Susan, is this yours?" I showed it to her.

"No, mine's at home on my bracelet."

"Mom," I said, "what is this?" I handed it to her.

"Oh, my," she said. "I'd forgotten all about that." She picked it up. It was a tiny gold charm, a graduation cap.

"What's the deal?" I said.

"Dad saw those one year when we were on vacation. He bought one for each of you—to give you when you graduated from college. He loved the little tassles that moved. When you dropped out of college to put Eliot through . . . " Mom shrugged her shoulders. "I guess he just forgot about them." She paused. "Well, he didn't forget them, because he remembered to give Susan hers when she graduated, but, well . . . " She shrugged her shoulders again.

I held out my hand and Mom put the little gold charm in my palm. I stared at it thoughtfully for a long while, then dangled it back and forth as I watched the tiny tassle quiver over the edge of the mortarboard. I handed it back to Mother.

By noon we had sorted through most of Daddy's things. Mom made tuna sandwiches for lunch and we finished eating a chocolate cake someone had brought over after the funeral.

"I think I'll go for a walk," I said. "I still have time before the kids get home from school." I looked at Mom. "Why don't you take a nap? You look tired."

"I think I will," she said, then paused. "Should we have waited? Maybe Uncle Arthur could have used Walter's clothes."

I shook my head. "I think it's best to give them to Goodwill," I said. I didn't want to see Uncle Arthur walking around in my father's clothes. Mother nodded her head, but there was a set to her shoulders that proclaimed she was still not sure we were doing the right thing. Stubbornness? Or indecision?

Mother went into the bedroom to lie down, and Susan settled on the couch with a book. I let myself out the back door and, without asking myself where I was going, I headed for my apple tree. It would be in bloom soon—beautiful pale pink blossoms hanging on the limbs, heavy with life. I stared at my branch with its wide gentle cradle, and then I pulled myself up into the tree. I felt shaky as I crept along the branch to my favorite spot. I used to scamper up the tree like a squirrel, without even thinking about it. Now I had to calculate each move—balancing myself anew each time I moved a leg. I sighed in relief as I settled my back against the branches and shifted my body into the V the limbs had formed, just for me.

College. I'd disappointed Dad. And I'd never known it. Had no idea. That explained his resentment of Eliot, so carefully masked. *When you dropped out . . . to put Eliot through.* But it was my decision, not Eliot's. No need to blame Eliot. No reason for a girl to go to college. You don't need college to be a wife and mother. No higher calling.

I plucked a twig from a nearby branch and stared at the tiny bud. In a few months it would be a fragile, pink blossom. I bent the twig between my fingers until it snapped. No smell. It had always disappointed me that the blossoms, so pale and delicate, had no aroma. They should smell sweet and overpowering, like a gardenia. The smell of life alone, the unembellished promise of the fruit to come, was a disappointment.

Everything was a disappointment. The answers no longer fit the questions. I had learned all the big answers before I'd faced the questions. Now, when I faced the questions for real—when I woke up each morning in reality asking "Why am I here?" really wanting an answer, really not knowing—the old answers didn't seem to fit. They appeared stale and outmoded. Lifeless. Maybe not lifeless. Maybe just unacceptable.

I stared at the broken twig in my fingers, then thrust it to the ground in frustration.

How long could we go on? How long could Eliot and I live side by side within a shell of a marriage? Months had passed already—a span of nothingness—and the future promised only more of the same. How long now? Eliot's birthday. It was easy to keep track of the date. Would it always be like that? From now on would I always mark time as Before and After? Like B.C. and A.D.? Like Before the Fall and After the Fall? What would I think seven years from now on Eliot's birthday? Seven years ago today I discovered . . .

CHAPTER 14

THE illusion of spring disappeared. April was wet and dreary. It was May before it seemed like spring again. Then May tiptoed past, and before I knew it school was out. As he had promised, Eliot began remodeling the bathroom. As soon as the work started, the quibbling began. The first thing we argued about was the bathtub. It was the old-fashioned kind with the claw feet. I loved it. Eliot hated it.

For some irrational reason it reminded me of Miss Emily, Faulkner's eccentric spinster. I couldn't remember the whole story, but things kept reminding me of her. There was something about her lover disappearing after threatening to leave her. And there had been talk of her trouble with rats—rat poison. For awhile there was a horrible stench around her house. Years later, when Miss Emily died, they had found the corpse of her lover on a bed in one of the upstairs bedrooms. On the pillow next to the body—or was it a skeleton by then?—were several long white hairs. Her hair had been vibrant brown at the time her lover had disappeared. When she died it was snowy white. She had been sleeping with his corpse all those years. Strange, very strange. I was strange to keep thinking about her. I wasn't sure where the bathtub fit in. Well, if she had a bathtub, it would have had legs, that was the connection. Weak—it was a weak connection.

"It has character," I said.

"That's not character, that's rust."

"Eliot, I love it. If you get rid of it, I'll scream."

"I don't understand what you see in it. It reminds me of cockroaches and food stamps."

"Cockroaches. You wouldn't recognize a cockroach if you saw one."

He leaned forward and peered down the drain hole. "Maybe not, but I know this is the sort of thing they'd like to scamper around in."

But I won. The tub stayed. It was the first of many such victories. I couldn't believe one small bathroom could involve so many choices. And if there was a choice there was an argument. We disagreed about the Formica, floor tile, and light fixtures. We even argued over what color toilet paper would look best when it was all finished.

The Portland Trailblazers made it to the NBA finals that spring, and the entire state was crazy with Blazermania. Eliot was no exception. He planned his work on the bathroom between the games on television. When the games came on, the work stopped. It was unfortunate that the final rash of games came when he had the sink, shower, and bathtub disconnected. We were two weeks with no shower or bathtub. Like everything else, we argued about where we should take our baths. Eliot and the children felt comfortable at Marlene's. I felt most comfortable at Mom's. Eliot thought we should all go to the same place.

"It just seems like we ought to at least be able to agree on taking our baths at the same house. Honestly, you going all the way out to the farm, the kids and I going to Tom's—it seems silly."

"What is this—the family that bathes together, stays together?"

Eliot looked drained. He was in awe of adages, proverbs, and all those little plaques that hung on my mother's walls. "Anything might help," he said quietly, more to himself than to me.

One afternoon I paused in the bathroom doorway and stared at the pipes, couplings, and clamps spread across the floor. "Why don't you have a plumber do this?" I queried.

"Why should I pay someone else to do it? I can figure it out."

"But you don't know a thing about plumbing."

"It's just like fixing a car—you put things back in the same order you take them out."

I didn't have much confidence in Eliot's ability to fix cars either, but I let that pass. "What's that?" I said, pointing to a short pipe with a handle on it.

"That's the thing that turns off the water."

"But what's it called?"

"I don't know. It hooks onto that straight pipe there, and then into that little round doohickey on the floor."

I felt panic rising in my throat. Eliot treated pipes the way he treated people. It was not important to him to know their names. I couldn't imagine putting the toilet together and not knowing that the round doohickey was called a floor flange.

I closed my eyes and pondered whether to put Eliot's peculiarity about names into the Fit or Don't Fit column of the chart I kept in my head. I was trying to analyze his personality. Which column? It didn't really matter. I just wanted it on one side or the other so I could label him and put him away. It was no good putting something in storage if it was uncatalogued. It was important to label Eliot.

But putting a tag on Eliot's character traits wasn't as easy as I had hoped. Love and hate battled inside of me, and putting him into storage was proving to be a ticklish undertaking. It was like trying to close the lid of a trunk stuffed with old clothes and photographs. I was trying to squeeze too many things into too small a space. Sleeves of old costumes kept slipping out. Photographic images of the past caught my attention just as I was bringing down the lid, and like a grandmother sorting through the attic, I paused to reminisce.

But it was not just the past that tied me to Eliot. We were still husband and wife. The glue of our marriage kept sticking to my feet and clinging to my elbows. We were like two old photographs which had become stuck to each other and then pulled apart. Images from one photo were superimposed upon the other. It was impossible to put them back the way they'd been before becoming fused. And our children walked around as living images of our cohesion. Tyler, with

Eliot's curly hair and my round eyes, was a haunting picture of all the things, some mysterious, some humdrum, that refused to disappear, that refused to deny our togetherness.

One Friday evening after the children were in bed, I prowled through the living room looking for a book I had been reading. Eliot was on the couch watching television. In my search I turned toward the sofa. I saw Eliot's rumpled curly hair and his eyes with their hint of pain. His velour robe was tied carelessly and his hairy legs were crossed—his right ankle resting across his left knee. I wondered why it was most men crossed their legs that way while preachers and politicians crossed theirs at the knees, like women, and why it was I preferred the ankle-knee arrangement. Eliot, apparently sensing me watching him, turned his eyes from the television. I looked into his eyes.

I'd never been able to resist them—the barely discernible drawing in of tiny muscles when he was lonely, and, in moments of passion, the mysterious flash of red. We stared at each other across the room. His eyes burned into mine. Even from across the room they sparked with power. Images from the past surrounded me and the loneliness of the present overwhelmed me. I was caught in the sticky mess of our garbled marriage.

Eliot raised his arm in slow motion and beckoned me toward him. I could not feel my body moving, but the space between us disappeared and I yielded myself into his arms. He gripped my shoulders, pulling my body closer to his. I felt the soft velour of his robe against my face and I clutched part of the sleeve between my fingers.

The glow from the television sprinkled our bodies with phosphorescent light. We moved together in the flickering blueness while the local newscaster and his sidekick, a young woman with a throaty chuckle, bantered back and forth about the Portland Trailblazers.

Later I lay in bed beside Eliot and could not sleep. I turned on the bedside lamp. Remembering I had been looking for my book earlier, I returned to the living room to search for it. I found the book beneath the couch.

I crept back to the stairway. Light from the streetlamp filtered through the leafy branches of the maple tree and streamed through the leaded glass windows along the stairwell. I paused a moment and looked through the windows toward the college campus, barely visible in the distance. I could identify the lights of the administration building and knew that the library was to the left and the humanities building on the right. I tightened my fingers around the book in my hand and snaked my way to the top of the stairs and into our bedroom.

Eliot was lying flat on his back, his head tilted upward, his mouth ajar. He didn't snore, but the sound of his sleep was familiar to me, and unmistakable. I saw the white of his neck and the black stubble of what I imagined would be a thick, curly beard, if he ever decided to grow one. I saw the pulse beating beneath his pale skin. As I stared at Eliot's white throat, I suddenly realized that the true intimacy of sleeping together had little to do with sex. It had to do with trust. *I could kill him,* I thought. *I could kill him in his sleep and he would never know what happened.*

Tears burned in my eye sockets, then coursed down my cheeks. After turning out the light, I slipped into bed beside Eliot and cried myself to sleep.

CHAPTER 15

THE Trailblazers won the NBA Championship that spring. A fresh wave of Blazermania swept across Oregon, leaving a wake of disbelief. Even Eliot, who had maintained for two years that the Blazers would take the NBA, was dumbfounded. "We're the champions," he said again and again. "I can't believe it—we're the champions."

Once the play-off games were over, work on the bathroom picked up. The old bathtub, standing proudly on its sturdy legs, in what once had been the linen closet, was once again serviceable. In spite of my misgivings, Eliot had managed to install a new sink as well as relocate the toilet. When you pushed the handle the toilet flushed, and when you turned on the faucet water came out. The bathroom was far from finished, but it was functional.

Eliot puttered his way through the first two weeks of July. By the third week work had slowed down again. Eliot's new responsibilities as head of the history department began to weigh on him, and he began spending time each day at the college. He also had hours of paperwork at home.

By the first week in August, work on the bathroom had come to a halt. I realized it was not going to get done. Not that summer, anyway. Whereas before I had been irritated by torn linoleum and exposed pipes, now I was irritated by torn linoleum and exposed studs. Everything worked beautifully, but it was ugly. It was ugly as blazes.

One morning after Eliot had left for the college, I went into the bathroom to brush my teeth. As I was leaving, I caught my robe on a protruding nail. I felt the pull, heard the rip, and turned to see the jagged gash in my beloved robe—my faithful, familiar, comfortable robe. As I stared at the slash, the reservoir of anger and frustration overwhelmed me. It was a moment when everything bad presented itself at one time and everything good did not exist. I was furious and frustrated and felt like I had spent my entire life being victimized by can openers, teachers, preachers, parents, ropes, my husband, children, and nails. Everyone but me determined my existence. I supposed that even God moved me around like a pawn on a chessboard and I was tired of it. I was sick and tired of it. I slammed my fist against the open studs and got a sliver. That made me angrier still.

Something was going to change. I didn't know what—but something.

I trudged into the kitchen and leaned against the counter. *If I had absolute control of my own life and could do anything in the world I wanted to do, what would it be?* I shook my head. I didn't know. What did I like to do? I rested my chin in my hands. I didn't know. I didn't have any idea.

I dashed up the stairs to get dressed. As I came back down the steps I noticed the children sitting in front of the television with the familiar vague looks on their faces.

"Shelly," I said, "vacuum and dust the living room. Do the stairway too."

"Mom—"

"Don't argue, Shelly, just do as I say."

"Gee whiz."

"Shelly!"

"Oh, all right."

"Matthew, you need to mow the lawn this morning. Don't forget to trim the edges."

"What about Tyler? What's Tyler going to do?"

"Tyler's coming with me."

"Where are you going?"

"To Alison's."

"That figures."

I didn't know if he was disgusted because Tyler was escaping his share of the work or because I was dashing off to Alison's, and I didn't care enough to ask. "Just be sure it's done by the time I get home," I said.

MOST of Milford was flat, streets and yards dividing it into dull, square parcels. The majority of the yards were landscaped predictably, as if someone had stood in the middle of the street and directed the effort. Kidney-shaped patches of grass were surrounded by areas of bark dust studded with shrubs and an occasional tree. Low window, low shrub. Bare wall, tall shrub. Colorful in May—rhododendrons and azaleas in bloom.

Alison's yard was different. From the street it was pleasant, but it lacked the studied order of nearby yards. As I stood in Alison's front room and looked out the window, I realized for the first time that her yard had been designed to be enjoyed from the inside out—not from the middle of the street.

It was like a quiet grove of trees with ferns and moss-covered rocks scattered amidst the shadowed quiet. The leaves of the trees quivered in the summer air while their shadows danced across the soft earth that was covered with delicate tendrils of ground cover and patches of wild flowers. I suspected it took a lot of work to keep it looking so natural, but I preferred to think it all just happened. When an image of Alison, her upper lip beaded with perspiration, her hands encased in grubby canvas gloves, pushed itself into my mind, I forced it aside, concentrating instead on the bright soft green of the moss against the crumbling gray of stone.

"Isn't it beautiful?" Alison said behind me, startling me a little.

"Yes, it is," I said. I resisted the impulse to ask if it was a lot of work. "It is beautiful."

Tyler disappeared into the playroom with Alison's two boys, and I followed Alison into the kitchen, where she fixed us each a cup of coffee. Alison was still wearing her robe and slippers. She looked comfortable and relaxed.

"I tore my robe this morning," I said.

"You tore your robe?"

"On a nail."

"Hmm."

"In the bathroom. There was a nail sticking out from the wall, and I tore my robe on it."

Alison was looking at me strangely, and I realized she didn't understand the significance of what I was saying. I sat at the table and rested my chin in my hands. "You see, Eliot hasn't finished the bathroom." I heaved a sigh and leaned back in my chair, folding my arms and tapping the fingers of my right hand against the upper part of my left arm. "He's not going to get it done this summer. It works, but that's all. He hasn't even put up the Sheetrock."

Alison placed a mug of coffee before me. "You're angry," she said.

"I'm furious."

She nodded her head. "I don't blame you."

"Alison," I said, waving my mug in the direction of our neighborhood, "I'm not staying in the house all winter with an unfinished bathroom."

"Well, that's interesting," she said. "Just what do you plan to do?"

I rested my chin in my hands again. "I don't know."

We sat in silence for a few minutes while I swirled my coffee mug in a tiny circle, watching the brown liquid slosh against the sides. I shrugged my shoulders. "I could finish it myself, I guess."

Alison threw her hands in the air. "Oh, sure. You think you've got nails sticking out of the walls now!" She poured us each another cup of coffee. "Why don't you hire someone to finish it?"

I stared at her in horror. "Hire someone! Are you kidding? Eliot would kill me. Besides, we can't afford it." I shook my head. "No, I could never do that." I leaned forward. "I think if I just had something else to do—to think about—if I wasn't just locked up in the house with that stupid bathroom all day long, maybe it wouldn't bother me so much."

"Like what?"

I stared into the distance. "I don't know. Well, like going back to school, maybe."

"Going to school?"

"Well, yes. I've been thinking about it anyway." I stared into my coffee mug. "When we went through my father's things we came across a little charm he had bought for me. It was a graduation cap. He had intended to give it to me when I graduated from college." I shook my head. "I had no idea he was counting on my graduating. I don't know—it just makes me feel kind of funny, like I let him down somehow."

"Did he act like you'd disappointed him?"

"No, not really. Although he did seem to resent Eliot—I quit to put Eliot through. I don't know. Maybe it wasn't that. But he did seem to resent him."

Alison leaned forward, her elbows on the table. "What was your father like? Did you always try to please him?"

I leaned back in the chair and crossed my legs. "I suppose so," I said. "Well, why not? He was a good father—a little insensitive sometimes—but usually more with Mom than with Susan and me. It was fun to please him because he was quick to lavish approval on us when we did. And he was thoughtful—really thoughtful, in lots of ways." As I spoke I realized Alison was one of the few people who had asked me anything about Father since he had died. I rarely spoke of him to anyone—except Mother, of course. She talked about him a lot. "Why shouldn't I want to please him?" I said.

Alison was thoughtful. "It's just that—well, if you go back to school because you want to, that's one thing, but if you're doing it to please your father—" She leaned forward. "It really doesn't do much good to live our lives to please others—they are rarely satisfied anyway. But when the person we're trying to please is dead—" She shrugged her shoulders. "Well, then it really is hopeless."

"I always loved school," I said. For some reason I felt angry and I could hear the defensiveness in my voice. "Maybe it's just what I need."

"Maybe so."

CHAPTER 16

AFTER my visit with Alison I sat around for days staring at the walls, mulling over the different things I could do to change my life-style. It suddenly seemed important to me to know what I really wanted out of life. Maybe it was because Alison made me realize it was too late to please my father, and I already knew it was impossible to please Eliot. Whatever the reason, I began considering my options. I supposed I could look for a job, but when I thought of different jobs I couldn't conjure up any that seemed worth doing. There was always volunteer work, but that didn't appeal to me either. In the end, going back to school was the only idea that caused a stir of excitement within me. And the more I thought about it, the more excited I became.

I announced my decision to Eliot at the breakfast table one morning.

"I'm going to finish college," I said.

"That's nice. Pass the sugar, please."

That's nice, pass the sugar? I passed him the sugar.

"I mean it," I said.

"Uh-huh." He was reading the newspaper.

"How much is tuition at Milford?"

"Not too bad—compared to some of the bigger schools." He was still reading the paper and his answer was automatic, his brain disengaged.

"Can we afford it? If I go back to school will you pay for it?"

"Uh-huh."

"You're sure? Because I mean it."

"Hmm."

I focused my eyes on Eliot and narrowed them as I watched him reading the paper. "Good," I said, smiling and rubbing my palms together.

A FEW weeks later Eliot walked into the kitchen and glanced at his watch. "I'm late," he said.

I placed his orange juice on the table and then his three-minute egg and buttered toast. Eliot cracked open his egg. "You cooked it too long again."

"I cooked it exactly three minutes."

"It's almost hard. You weren't paying attention."

"I did pay attention. I cooked it exactly three minutes."

Eliot shook his head, dropped his shoulders, and sighed.

"I have to register for classes today," I said as I poured him a cup of coffee.

"Hmm."

"I'll need some money."

Eliot looked up from the newspaper. "What did you say?"

"I have to register today. I'll need the money for tuition."

He laid down his newspaper. "You mean you're really going through with this?"

"I told you I was."

"Well, I thought you were just talking."

"I wasn't just talking. I meant it."

He scratched his head. "That's a lot of money, Rebecca."

"Eliot," I said, pressing my back against the kitchen counter, "I asked you if we could afford it and you said we could." My voice was rising. Suddenly I felt panicky. What if he wouldn't pay my tuition?

"Sometimes you start things and don't finish them, you know. If you want to do this, fine. But I don't want to put out all this money and then have you change your mind."

I pinched my lips together and gripped a drawer handle with my left hand—gripped it so tightly I could feel the metal design making a curlicue mark on my palm. "I'm not going to change my mind," I said firmly.

"How much do you need?"

"Well, I'm not sure."

Eliot put down his fork. "How can I write you a check if you don't know how much you need?"

"Why don't you just give me the checkbook?"

"Can you just figure out how much you need and tell me?"

"Well, I have. But I'm afraid there will be a charge for something I don't know about and then I won't have any money. Besides, there are books and all that—"

Eliot opened his checkbook and took his pen from his shirt pocket. "How much is tuition?"

I clenched my hands into hard little fists and told him. He wrote out the check, signing his name with the usual flourish.

"There," he said, handing it to me. Then he said something under his breath about stopping at the bank to transfer money from our savings account.

"What about my books?"

Eliot's tone was patiently impatient. "There'll be a list posted in the bookstore. Find out what you need and come up to my office. I'll write you another check." Eliot held the checkbook in the palm of his hand for a moment before he slipped it into his shirt pocket. I imagined Sir Galahad had held the Holy Grail in much the same manner.

"What if you're not there?"

"Then wait till I get there, OK?"

My cheeks felt flushed. "What if I don't feel like waiting?"

Eliot drank his orange juice in one long swallow and set the glass on the tabletop. It made a *thwack* sound when it hit.

"Do you want to go to school or not?" he said.

"Yes."

"Then please—just come to my office and I'll write you a check."

Thwack. Impatience. At the same time Eliot's impatience registered in my mind another realization zoomed into focus. I didn't care. I didn't care if he was impatient. I didn't care if he went into a paroxysm of rage and had a heart attack. All I cared about was getting registered for classes and starting school. Fear of Eliot's anger no longer paralyzed me into inaction. The tidings that Eliot's anger no longer touched me reached my soul and my heart sang with new freedom.

I was excited as I stepped onto the campus of Milford Junior College the first day of classes. But I still longed for a campus with shady trees and ivy-covered buildings. I seesawed between feeling superior and inadequate. By the time I arrived at my first class, I was a nervous wreck. I was horrified by the possibility that the seats were assigned and I was sitting in someone else's chair. Impossible. How could they possibly be assigned ahead of time?

But was I in the right room? I glanced at the other students to see if they had copies of *The Perrin-Smith Handbook of Current English*. I had checked the room number twice, but, unfamiliar as I was with the classroom facilities, it was possible I had the right room number but the wrong building. Finally I turned to the girl next to me and said, "Is this Composition 127?"

"This is the place," the girl replied. Then she resumed her conversation with a friend on the other side. I sighed, took out my notepad and ballpoint pen, transferring the blue plastic cap from the writing end to the other end, and with my pen poised for action, waited for my college career to resume.

By the time I entered my 1:00 class, Speech 122, I knew what to expect and was no longer worried about sitting in someone else's chair.

But speech class meant talking in front of people. I was terrified.

I turned to the boy seated on my right. "If I live through this class I can do anything," I said. As I spoke I realized I was conversing with someone akin to a Hell's Angel. I was as surprised to be talking to one as to realize there were any still around. I thought the Hell's Angels had gone the way of the Flower Children—they turned thirty.

His face was covered by a dark beard. His long wavy hair was pulled back in a ponytail, and he wore a faded denim jacket and ragged jeans.

"I know what you m-mean," he replied. His eyes were kind, and I hoped the fact he wore an earring in one of his ears didn't mean what I thought it meant. He spoke with a slight stutter, and I realized he had more reason to fear speech class than I did.

I shifted my eyes to his hiking boots. They reminded me of the ones I had bought for Matthew when he was three. Matthew's had had eight eyelets, and it had taken him aeons to get them laced each morning. I started counting the eyelets on his boots but stopped when he noticed me staring at them.

"I'll bet your mother hates those boots," I said. "They track dirt all over the floors."

The minute the words were out of my mouth I was sorry. It was exactly the housewifey type of comment I had been determined not to make.

"You're right," he replied, "she does."

I stared at him in surprise. I didn't know which one of us was more embarrassed—me, for being a mother, or him, for having one.

"Are you a Hell's Angel?" I asked, trying for a half-serious, half-mocking tone.

His eyes crinkled at the corners and again I noticed the kindness in them. "No," he said.

His name was Jesse, and after that first day we always sat next to each other. We had been drawn together by fear, a bond of mutual fear, but after a few weeks our fear melted away and was replaced by a sense of challenge and self-satisfaction. Through listening to each other's speeches, we found we asked the same questions of life. I gave speeches about making choices—choices between good and bad, hope and defeat. Jesse gave eloquent speeches dealing with reality and illusion. He never stuttered during his speeches. In fact, they were practically flawless. But he would plop into his desk afterward, lean over and say, "H-how did I d-do?"

Although Jesse and I asked the same questions of life, neither of us had come up with many answers—at least not many new answers, and the old ones no longer worked. We were like searching, weary pilgrims on a quest for truth. We were grateful for company along the way—even strange company.

After a few weeks of school, I was surprised to realize that Sidney

Wolfe's speech class was my favorite. Eliot had warned me about Sidney, who liked to think of himself as innovative. Eliot said he was off-the-wall.

"He'll try anything as long as it's new or weird," Eliot had said. "But he has one pet peeve I can identify with."

"What's that?"

"He can't stand criers."

"Criers?"

"Criers—students who burst into embarrassed sobs if they mess up a speech."

I had winced at Eliot's words.

Sidney Wolfe had stood in front of the class on that first afternoon and had scanned the faces before him. His eyes had rested a moment on me. I hoped it was because he recognized me as Eliot's wife and not because I had the earmarks of a crier. *Eliot's wife. The woman betrayed. Did he know that? Did everyone know that? Paranoid. Don't be paranoid.*

In spite of Sidney's weirdness, or maybe because of it, his class remained my favorite. Students got to know each other better in that class than in the others. Besides, I had discovered I enjoyed being in front of an audience—feeling their response to me and to the things I shared with them. I especially loved the critique sessions marked by long debates and runaway emotions.

I prided myself on keeping my cool and I was delighted when others lost theirs.

CHAPTER 17

ONE afternoon, several weeks into fall term, Sidney was shuffling the papers on his desk and clearing his throat. He always cleared his throat when he wanted the class to settle down. There was a movement in the doorway and I looked up to see Jesse. After hesitating slightly, he slipped into the empty chair next to mine. Sidney was still clearing his throat and rearranging the items on his desk.

"You weren't here Tuesday," I said.

"Did you m-miss me?"

I stared at him a moment. "Yes," I said. He laughed. I knew he was laughing because of the surprise in my voice.

"I didn't f-feel like getting up," he said, shrugging his shoulders, "so I didn't."

"Very commendable," I said.

"You disapprove?"

I didn't want to sound like Old Mother Hubbard. I shrugged my shoulders. "No, no. You can stay in bed all day if you want to." I lowered my head and felt vaguely uncomfortable.

"I'm just l-like that some days," he said. "I give myself permission not to g-get up."

"That's fine," I said, still feeling uncomfortable. I slouched lower in my chair and leaned toward Jesse as he spoke.

"It's just that—"

"I'm being distracted," boomed Sidney Wolfe from the front of the room. Sidney had been trying to begin the lesson. I smiled sheepishly. Sidney glowered at us a moment longer and then, after clearing his throat one final time, began the day's lecture.

SIDNEY Wolfe's afternoon speech class was the last class of the day for both Jesse and me, and we fell into the habit of visiting for awhile afterward. Some days we plopped onto the chairs in the hallway outside the classroom and visited there, while the rooms filled and emptied around us. Other students nodded as they passed on their way into class, and then nodded again on their way out—startled little nods at finding us still there. One day we leaned against two white posts near the parking lot and visited until we were both tired of standing. We tried sitting on the posts, but they were only four inches across and didn't make good stools. We shifted around on them uncomfortably until it was time for me to leave.

Most of the time we went to the campus snack shop for a cup of coffee. "I'll meet you there," Jesse said one day after class. "I need to turn in this requisition to the audiovisual department."

As I entered the coffee shop I headed for the corner table on the left. Somebody was already there. I was annoyed—and surprised at my annoyance. It hadn't occurred to me before that we always sat at that corner table. I bought a cup of coffee for each of us and carried them to a table near the center of the room. When Jesse arrived he plopped into the chair opposite me with a sigh. "Someone has our t-table," he said. He brushed his ponytail away from his shirt collar as he spoke.

"I know," I said. I was only a little surprised that he also considered the corner table ours.

It was Jesse's idea to take Sidney Wolfe's evening workshop—Interpersonal Communication. I told Eliot it was an easy way to pick up credit hours, and it was, but I didn't pretend to myself that was my only motive. I just liked the idea of exploring personal relationships in a class with Jesse and Sidney. Jesse's searching mind continued to delight me, and any class of Sidney's was sure to be interesting. Bizarre maybe.

The class ran for three weeks, four nights a week. Three credit hours.

I didn't realize how upsetting a night class would be to our family schedule. I came home from school in the afternoon already tired, and when I thought about fixing dinner and rushing out to my seven o'clock class, I was so overwhelmed I resorted to TV dinners.

"Rebecca, this has been rough," Eliot said after the third night. "When are you going to cook us a decent meal?"

I stared at him, managing to feel hurt. "I don't see what you're complaining about," I said. "We had chicken Monday night, Swiss steak Tuesday. I mean, it's not as if we're having the same thing night after night."

Eliot rolled his eyes to the ceiling. "Three hundred and sixty-five ways to eat cardboard."

I ignored him.

Night after night I walked out of the kitchen leaving behind an irritated husband, perplexed children, and a pile of dirty dishes—if you can call five forks, five glasses, and five aluminum trays a pile of dirty dishes.

On Monday night, the second week of the workshop, Jesse didn't show up for class. We had planned to go out for coffee afterwards and I was tempted to leave class to call him. But I didn't know his phone number. I supposed it might be listed in the phone book. But for some reason it was incomprehensible to me that someone like Jesse, with his ponytail and earring, would have his phone number listed like everyone else.

I knew what Eliot would say. *"Look on the wall in the men's room."* Eliot didn't approve of Jesse.

"We're going to do some soft body work tonight," Sidney said. In my anxiety over what he meant by soft body work I forgot about Jesse. "I want each of you to find a spot along the wall and lie down with your feet against the wall, head resting on one arm, the other hand clamped on the top of your head." I stared at Sidney Wolfe. How had I ever gotten myself into this? "I want you to lean forward and inhale, then lean back and exhale. In and out. Open and closed. OK? Find your spots."

After one week of classes I knew I wasn't the most inhibited member of the group. The knowledge surprised me and left me with a feeling akin to responsibility. I shoved back my chair and noticed that immediately others began moving about—hesitant moves toward an exercise we all considered ridiculous. *Maybe I'm a leader,* I thought.

I took my place on the floor, curled up into a tiny ball, and took a deep breath. Then I uncurled and released the air. In and out. In and out. When I was curled up I felt closed and safe, like behind my wall—safe from Eliot's betrayal and safe from the eyes that had looked into another's. But after awhile my lungs felt too full of air and I felt strangled. I needed to move. I needed to open up. When I leaned back and let the air out of my lungs, I saw a shaft of light, like the one in Eliot's eyes, and I saw us laughing together at his black socks, laughing and laughing, our mouths open, our throats white and exposed. As I concentrated on my own exposed throat, vulnerable and trembling, my laughter turned to tears. I took a deep breath and curled up into myself again. I wanted to stay there, closed and safe—trapped inside myself, impregnable.

I repeated the exercise again and again. Each time it was the same—the security of being closed in was eventually stifling, but the joy of being open filled me with terror.

"OK," Sidney said softly, "now get up slowly and form a circle on the floor." Sidney talked in hushed tones and we all moved slowly, as if we were in a trance and afraid that any sudden movement would dispel it. "Let's talk about how you felt during the exercise."

We slithered into a ragged circle around Sidney.

"What are some reactions?" he whispered.

I stared at Sidney. *Keep quiet, Rebecca. Don't say anything.*

I cleared my throat. "I—I felt a real conflict inside," I said.

Sidney was watching me closely, and I could feel moisture gathering around my eyes. *Don't cry. Don't cry. Sidney Wolfe can't stand criers.*

"What kind of conflict?" Sidney asked. His voice was gentle and he didn't act like he hated criers.

"Well, I wanted to stop rocking. I wanted to stay one way or the other—open or closed." I paused, blinking my eyes rapidly. "It seemed to tie in somehow with a conflict about—about whether to share myself with—with, well, share myself."

Sidney stared at me and I shifted uneasily. *Eliot. My wall. A woman betrayed. Does Sidney know that?* I moved my legs to a more comfortable position.

"I'm not sure I understand," he said.

Maybe not. Maybe he doesn't know.

"Well, I don't know exactly. Being closed up was kind of like holding everything inside—anger, fear, love even. Being open was like—well, like letting everything hang out. You know, here I am world, take it or leave it. If you don't like me the way I am you can . . ." I shrugged my shoulders.

Sidney stared at me for a moment then cleared his throat. "Rebecca has touched upon something quite important regarding communication. Can anyone tell me what it is?"

I lowered my head and stared at the floor. What had I touched upon? Why didn't someone say something? Several of the students shifted positions, but still no one spoke. Finally Sidney broke the silence. "I think some of the conflict Rebecca was feeling . . ."

I glared at him. I hated being referred to in the third person—like a specimen under a microscope.

" . . . has something to do with deciding whether or not we're going to trust another person, or people, with our private feelings."

"I don't get it," one of the students said.

"Well," Sidney said, looking more thoughtful than I had ever seen him, "if you decide to share your hidden self with someone, and they reject you, it can be devastating. At the very least it will be that much harder to share your feelings the next time. Very often the withdrawal begins in early childhood, before the person is consciously aware of it. Result: Withdrawn adult." With those final words Sidney tucked his head and drew his shoulders together, illustrating what a withdrawn adult looked like. It was a comic picture, we chuckled, and the seriousness of his words was dispelled.

As I watched Sidney, I realized he had been a little embarrassed by his own solemnity, and was eager to get back to his studied nonchalance. "Well," he said, taking a sip of coffee from the mug he always had nearby, "some other reactions. How did the rest of you feel during the exercise?"

AFTER class several of the students surrounded Sidney to ask questions or complain about the exercise. I winced inwardly as I raised myself from the floor. My legs had fallen asleep. In a desperate attempt not to limp or walk stiff-legged, I made my way back to my desk and retrieved my coat, purse, and book bag. As I belted my coat, Sidney glanced in my direction and our eyes met for an instant. Then he turned his attention back to the student talking to him. I slipped my book bag over my shoulder and headed for the door.

"Rebecca," Sidney said, still seated on the floor, "could you wait? I'd like to talk to you for a minute."

"Oh, OK." I said. "Sure." I stood still for a moment, then sat in a nearby chair. I watched Sidney answering questions and I could see he was conscious of me waiting and was anxious to dispense with the other students. I was anxious to see if he would have as hard a time getting up from the floor as I had.

After the last student left, I watched Sidney press his hand against the floor and push up with his arm as he slowly unfolded his legs. He did a funny little jump to force himself upright and then pressed the palm of his left hand against the small of his back. "Oh," he said, "I must have gotten a cramp." He shuffled toward me, holding his back and grunting his discomfort.

I smiled slightly. "That's too bad."

He plopped into the desk next to mine. He crossed his legs, his right ankle resting across his other knee, and began toying with his ragged shoelace. "I was interested in the conflict you talked about tonight," he said. "I struggle with that a lot myself." He twisted the shoelace around his index finger. "Do you have time to go to Bower's for a beer?"

"A beer?"

He shrugged his shoulders. "Well, it doesn't have to be a beer . . . a glass of wine, coffee?"

"Well, uh, sure, I guess so." I hesitated. "But I'll need to phone Eliot so he won't worry. Is there a phone around here?"

"There's one at Bower's. Why don't you call him from there?"

"Oh, OK."

"I'll meet you there," he said, "inside. There's a phone in the entryway."

Bower's Tower, on the corner of Second and Halsey, was an actual tower. It had originally been a mercantile center built by Harold Bower, one of Milford's more eccentric founding fathers. In recent years the lower level had been turned into a tavern. The atmosphere appealed to college students and had quickly become their favorite hangout, much to the consternation of college officials and local parents.

"I don't think he checks the ID of students very carefully," Marlene had complained one day at Bible study. "Tom says he has seen some of his freshmen staggering out of there."

I could imagine Marlene and Tom cuddled in bed at night dissecting the people who had come across their paths that day—mistaking gossip for intimacy.

As I walked across the parking lot toward the tavern, I wondered what quirk of old man Bower had inspired him to build a tower on the corner of Second and Halsey in Milford, Oregon.

Some fantasy about Rapunzel.

I glanced at the second-story windows, the ones where Rapunzel would have let down her tresses. Gold letters on the glass panes said Dr. Hemly, Dentist. The other window said No Appointment Necessary.

When I opened the heavy door of Bower's Tower and stepped into the entryway, I saw Sidney flirting with the cashier. The pay telephone was on the wall to my right.

"I'll be right with you," I said to Sidney. I headed for the telephone, fumbling in my purse for a quarter. "Oh, rats," I said. "Do you have a quarter?"

"Sure," he said. He fished in his pocket for his change and tossed me a quarter. "It's the least I can do for old Eliot," he said, winking. I stared at him a moment then turned away.

I pressed the quarter between my thumb and index finger as I stood before the phone and carefully read the directions. I'm always afraid they'll change them without my knowing.

"Eliot? This is Rebecca. . . . No, no, I'm OK. Listen, I'm going to be a little late tonight. Huh? Oh, some of us are going out for coffee after class. No, you don't need to wait up. . . . OK, good-bye."

"Is everything OK?" Sidney asked, as we walked into the smoky tavern.

"Sure," I said, "everything's fine."

We sat at a little drop-leaf table, and when our waiter approached I thought for a moment it was Jesse—denim overalls, ponytail, and, yes, one gold earring. I glanced at his feet. At least he wasn't wearing those horrible boots. Nice soft moccasins. Much better. The waiter shifted his foot and as his moccasin slid across the floor a layer of dust filtered into the air and then drifted back to the rough planks, seeping comfortably into the cracks.

"Rebecca?"

"Huh?"

"What do you want?"

"Oh." I realized he was asking me for the second time. "Oh, just coffee, I guess." I lifted my chin and glanced at the waiter. "With cream—and don't forget the cream. I can't stand waiters who forget the cream." I smiled at him and he shrugged his shoulders.

"One coffee, one beer," he said, scribbling the order on a plain three-by-five notepad. "Got it." He shuffled toward the bar and I could hear the sound of the dirt on the floor scraping beneath his moccasins.

I glanced around the dark room, wondering if I would recognize, or be recognized by, any of the other customers. When my eyes returned to Sidney's face, he was smiling, amused by my concern.

In a few moments Jesse's twin set my coffee in front of me and handed a frosty mug of beer to Sidney. The waiter started to walk away and I stared at my coffee. "Hey," I said, "you forgot my cream." He sauntered off. He hadn't heard me. I sighed in frustration. "What is it with me? I can never get cream for my coffee."

"You need to be more assertive," Sidney said.

"I was assertive," I said. "I told him I couldn't stand waiters who forget the cream."

"Yeah, but you smiled."

"What?"

"You smiled. You said, 'I can't stand waiters who forget the cream.'" Sidney used a high-pitched voice. "Then you smiled sweetly." He smiled and batted his eyelashes. "You can't smile."

"Well, would you get him over here so I can get my cream?"

"No."

"What?"

"Get him over here yourself."

I stared at him. "How?"

"Well, how did you expect me to get him here?"

"I don't know." I shrugged my shoulders. "Whatever it is you do—snap your fingers or holler or something."

"You holler."

"I'll just drink it black."

"You mean you'd rather sit here and drink it black than get him to bring you what you ordered in the first place?"

"I drink it black sometimes."

"Right. When you're too chicken to ask the waiter for the cream."

I followed our waiter around the room with my eyes but he never looked in my direction. "Why does he have that earring in his ear?" I said.

"How should I know?"

"Well, isn't it supposed to mean something?"

"Like what?"

"Well, like maybe he's gay or something."

I took a sip of my black coffee and Sidney smiled in amusement. "I don't know. Is that what it means?"

"I don't know," I said, shrugging my shoulders. "I just heard that somewhere." I put my chin in my hands. "But then I also heard a gold earring in one ear helps you quit smoking." I coughed discreetly and Sidney moved the ashtray to the other side of the table, shaking his head.

"Are you really going to drink that coffee black?"

"Maybe he'll come by with a refill. I'll ask him then."

"They're offering a class in a few weeks."

"What kind of class?"

"Assertiveness."

"I don't need a class on assertiveness. I get along fine."

Sidney inhaled deeply on his cigarette and let the smoke out slowly. "If you're going to continue taking your coffee with cream," he said, "you'd better take the class."

I made a face at him and took another sip of the bitter coffee. "What did you want to talk to me about?" I said.

Sidney took a sip of his beer and a puff from his cigarette. He put his elbow on the table and the smoke from his cigarette blew across my face. "You seemed really upset by the exercise we did in class tonight. I wanted to make sure I hadn't started some horrible trauma."

"You didn't start it." I stared into my coffee.

"But it was traumatic." It was a statement, but Sidney's voice was edged with curiosity.

"Yes, it was traumatic." I took a sip.

Sidney stared at me a moment. "You don't want to talk about it?" Another declarative sentence punctuated by a question mark.

"I don't know." I scooted my chair back a little and crossed my legs. *Eliot. My wall. A woman betrayed.* I folded my arms and then unfolded them, leaning forward, my elbows on the table. I countered with a question of my own. "You said you had experienced the same kind of conflict. What did you mean?"

Sidney frowned and smashed his cigarette butt in the ashtray, squishing it back and forth with his finger until it was mangled, the little brown pieces of tobacco jutting through the thin white paper. "Just that conflict over whether or not it's safe to share me—you know, the inside me, with others."

"You teach the class," I said. "You say it again and again, take the risk, share yourself."

"Physician heal thyself."

"I almost started crying in class tonight."

"I know, that's why I was concerned about you."

"Before I signed up for your speech class, Eliot . . . Eliot warned me that one thing you can't stand is criers."

"Embarrassed criers I can't stand, the ones who cry just because they've blown a speech and humiliated themselves. You weren't embarrassed tonight, you were just—" Sidney held his hands toward me, "—emotional. I can put up with honest emotion."

"Other people's."

"Yeah, other people's."

"What are you afraid of?" I was eager to keep the conversation away from myself.

Sidney took out another cigarette and lit it ceremoniously. "I don't know. I feel like I have some deep well of ugliness inside me and if I start letting it out I won't be able to stop it. It will seep and ooze everywhere, making a mess I won't be able to clean up."

I nodded my head slowly and I could feel tears starting to form in my eyes again. I stared into my coffee and finally took a sip of the lukewarm black liquid. "Have you always felt that way?"

"I don't know. I guess I never used to notice it." He shrugged his shoulders. "I guess it was my divorce that made me face it. Elaine said I didn't share myself with her—didn't communicate." He shrugged his shoulders again.

"And you teach a class on interpersonal communication? Who plans the curriculum around here?"

"I can teach it," Sidney said, his voice trimmed in defense. "I have all the theory. I just can't live it. Besides, you know what they say about why psychiatrists become psychiatrists—this is the same thing."

"How long have you been divorced?"

"One year. One year next month."

"Hmm. Not very long."

He nodded his head, surprised. "Most people think one year is a long time."

I shook my head. "Nope." I spoke with the easy authority of non-experience. "It takes two years to get your head back together."

"How do you know? You've never been divorced."

"I read a lot."

"So do I," he said, shaking his head. "But it hasn't done much good." He took another drink of his beer. "But what about you? I didn't bring you to Bower's Tower to cry on your shoulder. What was troubling you tonight?"

I shook my head.

"You're not going to talk about it, huh?"

I rested my chin in my hands. "I guess it was just the realization that communication involves a choice. On what do we base that choice? How much risk is too much? Maybe I just don't want to take responsibility for my relationships. Just let them happen—see what develops."

Sidney smashed another cigarette butt into the ashtray. "That was my attitude with Elaine," he said. "Just wait and see what would develop." He picked up his mug of beer and moved it around slowly in a circle, staring into the miniature whirlpool. "A divorce developed," he said quietly. "That's what developed."

CHAPTER 18

SIDNEY started joining Jesse and me for coffee after speech class on Tuesdays and Thursdays. Eliot and I rarely saw each other on campus, but a few times he had spotted me in the coffee shop with Jesse and Sidney. One day he joined us.

Sidney had been trying to get me to enroll in his drama class the next term. "She's doing very well in speech," he said to Eliot. "She's probably my best student."

"She's not a crier?" Eliot said. He smiled at Sidney in a man-to-man way, suggesting that, after all, I didn't need to be taken seriously.

Sidney stiffened. "No, she's not." He smiled at me. "Not in speech class anyway."

I met his eyes briefly and turned to Eliot. "I enjoy it a lot," I said. I seldom talked about school to Eliot. He didn't really know which classes I enjoyed and which I didn't. He nodded his head without comment.

Sidney and Jesse continued an argument they'd begun earlier. Jesse presented his case timidly. "I think audience participation is f-fine," he said. "It gives the spectator a chance to really be a part of what's happening on stage."

Sidney was emphatic. "It may be all great fun, but it puts drama on the level of charades—it's no longer a viable art form."

"I don't see why you s-say that," Jesse said.

Sidney leaned forward and thumped his fist lightly on the table. "Aesthetic distance," he said. "Aesthetic distance is absolutely necessary if drama is to remain authentic."

I leaned forward eagerly. "What's aesthetic distance?"

Sidney sipped his coffee and puffed his ever-present cigarette. "It's what separates the audience from the action on the stage. It's a feeling of safety. Audience participation violates that safety—breaks down the illusion."

"Illusion?" I asked, leaning toward him. He sensed my interest and continued, smashing his cigarette into the ashtray with the usual violence.

"Nudity and sexual activity on the stage are good examples," he said. I could sense Eliot shifting in his chair, and I glanced in his direction. He looked at his watch. I turned back to Sidney. "When there is sexual activity on stage the audience usually slips from illusion to delusion—they don't know it's not real—because it is real. The audience knows the actor has to take part in it."

"But that's not audience participation," Jesse said. "That's something else."

Sidney tilted his hand from side to side. "I don't know," he said. "The audience loses distance in the same way that—"

Eliot glanced at his watch again and shoved back his chair. "You'll have to excuse me," he said. "I need to get back to my office. Rebecca, would you like to walk back with me?"

I glanced at his face. His jaw was set in that funny way it gets when he's angry. It had shifted to one side. "Oh, OK. Sure. I'll see you guys later."

"Think about that drama class," Sidney said. "I think you'd like it."

"I will. 'Bye."

Eliot took my elbow and led me toward his office. His shoulders were sloped forward and the soles of his boots crushed the grass as he tromped across the campus. "I don't believe you," he said as we approached the barracks-like structure.

"What?"

We stepped into Eliot's office building, and I smiled at the receptionist. I felt like a rebellious student being marched to the principal's office. What I wanted to do more than anything else was giggle.

Eliot's office was still a disappointment to me. The partitioned walls did not go all the way to the ceiling and it seemed unreal. A pretend room—like a mobile home seems like a pretend house.

Eliot closed the curtain door behind us. That was the worst part. His office didn't even have a door. It had a curtain—like the entrance to the stockroom in a dusty shoe store.

"Couldn't you at least wear a dress or something?" Eliot said.

I stared at him. Where was this man coming from?

"Well, look at you—jeans, tennis shoes, tee shirt—I don't know."

Eliot waved me into a molded plastic chair and I sat down. His fingertips galloped on the top of his desk without getting anywhere. "I can barely tolerate college freshmen when they're fresh-faced kids," Eliot said, "but when they're older women with puffy faces and round eager eyes—it's just ridiculous, that's all." Eliot caught the look on my face. "Oh, I don't mean you're one of those pasty-faced females. You look like one of the kids, with those old blue jeans and all, but I just hate to see you acting so—so typical."

I lifted my chin and stared across the make-believe office. Shifting my eyes back to Eliot, I looked right at him as I spoke. "You're just going to have to let me go through the same stages everyone else goes through, Eliot. If I seem ridiculous to you, I'm sorry. You'll just have to put up with it. I love school. I love what I'm learning and I'm not going to start wearing a dress or spend time worrying about acting like a typical college freshman. I don't mean to be acting like anything. I am a college freshman. For the first time in ages I am just being what I am." I leaned back and crossed my legs. I smiled, but I couldn't feel the smile in my eyes. "If you don't like it," I said, "you can stuff it."

"Rebecca!" He looked confused.

I glanced at my watch. "I was supposed to pick up Shelly five minutes ago." I searched in my bag for my car keys.

"But, Rebecca, well—OK. We'll talk some more tonight."

I stopped in the doorway, holding the curtain against the door frame with one hand while I continued to dig in my bag with the other. "I have a class tonight," I said, glancing only briefly at Eliot. "I won't be home until late." I could hear the self-satisfaction in my voice.

"I thought Thursday was your last workshop."

"It was. I've signed up for an assertiveness class."

Eliot's jaw dropped. "Assertiveness? Why in the world are you taking?—oh, my gosh."

I lifted my chin. "I'm going to learn how to get cream for my coffee."

A wry smile played at the corners of his mouth. "Why don't you try Home Ec?"

I didn't smile. I'd already learned how not to smile.

Eliot hesitated. "Well, what about dinner?"

"There are some TV dinners in the freezer."

He studied me a moment. "OK," he said at last. "OK."

AS I plowed through week after week of school—turning new thoughts over in my mind, preparing the ground for a new life—many of the things that had once been important to me fell by the wayside. I did housework sporadically and only when it was convenient. The closets were in shambles, and I never looked closely into corners.

One day I returned home from school in the late afternoon and rushed upstairs to freshen up for my evening class. Eliot followed me up the stairs and into the bedroom.

"I fed the kids early," he said. "I thought I'd broil steaks for us a little later." He paused. "I made some pudding for dessert."

"I don't have time to eat," I said without thinking, pawing through the closet for my yellow sweater. "I'm going to be late for class the way it is."

"You have class tonight?"

"Of course I have class tonight, Eliot. It's Thursday night. I always have class on Thursday."

"Oh, that's right." His shoulders drooped. "I forgot."

I didn't notice him leave the bedroom, but a few minutes later when I rushed through the kitchen and out the back door, I saw him sitting alone at the kitchen table, eating chocolate pudding out of one of our stemmed dessert dishes.

He looked pathetic. I couldn't help thinking about the evening I had cried into my Lemon Mist Dessert while he . . .

I didn't feel sorry for him.

SOMETIMES when I had a night class I stayed at the college through dinnertime. Usually I called. Sometimes I forgot. The refrigerator was often empty, and the children and Eliot learned to forage on their own. They set up a cooking and shopping schedule and created their own housekeeping rules. If I showed up for dinner, fine—if not, fine. I was no longer the hub around which the household revolved. Little by little, Eliot and the kids had been learning to fend for themselves.

"But Mom," Shelly complained one evening when I refused to do her laundry, "that's your job."

"What do you mean that's my job?"

"You're the mother, you're supposed to do the laundry."

"I wash my clothes. You can wash yours."

"But . . ."

"But what?"

Shelly threw her hands in the air. "I don't know—I don't even know how to do it."

"It's not all that hard, Shelly. It's time you learned, anyway. Just put the clothes in the washer, add the soap, and turn on the machine."

Shelly learned to do her own wash. The whites turned gray because she washed everything together, and the permanent press ceased to be permanent because she dried everything on hot, but they were washed.

One evening while I was doing my homework Matthew stood beside the table. "Mom, I don't have any clean shirts."

There had been a time when I would have been overjoyed to know Matthew recognized the difference between clean and dirty. Now, my only response was, "Hmm."

"Are you going to wash tomorrow?"

I didn't look up from my books. "Um, I don't know. I don't think so."

"But I need a clean shirt."

I lifted my head, "Matthew, please. I'm trying to study. Please don't bother me when I'm studying."

Eliot was standing in the doorway. "Come on, Matthew, Mommy's busy. Let's round up your dirty clothes. We can wash a load tonight and they'll be ready in the morning."

So it was that Eliot and the children began doing their own laundry.

It wasn't long before they had a fairly efficient system going and the family continued to appear civilized in the eyes of the community.

One afternoon I rushed into Eliot's office. "I forgot to tell you, Shelly has a dentist appointment this afternoon. You can take her, can't you?"

Eliot glanced up from his papers and then at his watch. "I have a department meeting this afternoon."

"Well, it shouldn't take too long. It's just a checkup."

"What time?"

"Three-thirty."

"The meeting starts at four—I'd never make it. I can't sneak in late, I'm conducting it."

"Typical," I said. "Just typical. You think nothing of asking me to change my schedule around. I'm just a woman. But you—you wouldn't think of making an adjustment to take care of the children. That's women's work." I'd forgotten the laundry, the dishes, and the cleaning Eliot had been doing. I'd forgotten Eliot had been called out of class take Matthew to the doctor for stitches when he'd fallen at recess and the school couldn't locate me. My voice was loud and Eliot glanced to the top of the partitioned walls, knowing I could be heard in the next three cubicles. Why didn't they give him a real office? He was head of the department. If he had a real office I could yell at him all I wanted.

"Do you have a class?" Eliot said, using his calmest voice.

"No, I have some research to do at the library."

"Can't you do it some other time?"

"I wanted to do it this afternoon."

Eliot stared at me. "You're not being reasonable, Rebecca."

"I don't care," I said. "It's time you started taking me seriously."

"I do take you seriously, but this afternoon I have a meeting that I cannot miss. You can do your research anytime. I'm willing to cooperate with you, Rebecca, if you'll just be reasonable. You're being ridiculous."

I glared at him. He was right. I knew he was right. There was no reason I couldn't do the research another time. But I was afraid to give in—afraid that if I gave in this time there would be another time, and then another. Pretty soon I would be right back where I started.

"It's the same old story," I said.

Eliot fastened his serious eyes on me. He shook his head. "No it's not, Rebecca. If you expect me to take you seriously, you're going to have to be rational. It is not sensible for me to miss my meeting just because you feel like doing your research—that's not reasonable."

Not reasonable . . . if you expect me to take you seriously . . . be rational.

I bit my lower lip. "OK," I said. "I suppose I can do it some other time." I paused. I knew how much Eliot disliked my being gone in the evening, so I tacked on a small victory for myself. "I'll come down to the library tonight and do it."

I saw his shoulders drop.

SHELLY was waiting for me on the front steps of the junior high. She hopped into the backseat. I checked the rearview mirror then pulled into the street. Shelly leaned forward.

"Mom?"

"Yeah?"

"Do we have a family tree?"

"Everyone has a family tree, Shelly."

"You know what I mean. I'm supposed to do a family tree for English class. It's due next week."

"Well, there's part of one in your baby book. I never finished it. Maybe Grandma Adamson could help you. I think she's interested in family trees."

"Adamson, Adamson. What does our name mean—Adamson?"

"I don't know. Son of Adam, I guess."

"Shelly Adamson—that's dumb."

"What?"

"I'm not a son. Why should I be called Adam's son?"

"Well, what do you want to be called? Shelly Evesdaughter?"

She folded her arms on the back of the seat and rested her chin on her wrists. "That would be a dumb name, I guess." Then she straightened her back and peered at me. "But it's more logical, don't you think?"

"These things defy logic."

"Well, it's stupid. Adamson."

"In a few years you'll get married and your name will change anyway, so what's the big deal?"

"Hmm." Shelly leaned toward me and checked her reflection in the rearview mirror, pulling her bangs back to check something about her eyebrows.

"Shelly, don't do that. I can't see what's going on behind me."

She scooted to the other side of the car and rested her chin on her arms again. "Mom?"

"Yeah?"

"What was your maiden name?"

"Shelly!"

"What?"

"You know my maiden name, good grief. Carter. Grandpa would turn over in his grave. What's my maiden name! Good grief. Rebecca Carter, Rebecca Anne Carter."

"Well, you don't have to get all upset."

"I'm not upset. I just can't believe you didn't know my maiden name."

"I forgot, that's all. I just didn't make the connection there for a minute."

Shelly nestled her chin lower onto the car seat and slouched her back, staring off into space. "Maybe when I get married I'll keep my maiden name," she said. "That way people won't forget who I really am."

"It won't do any good," I said. "It's your father's name. You're my daughter too, you know."

"Well, maybe I'll take your maiden name, then. Shelly Carter, that sounds nice."

"That was my father's name," I said.

"Well, what was your mother's maiden name?"

"Lorimer."

"Shelly Lorimer, then."

"But that was my mother's father's name."

She was silent a long time. Finally she said, "It would just go on and on, wouldn't it?"

"Hmm?"

"It would just go on and on. No matter how far back we went it would always be the father's name. How can we ever find out who we really are?"

"What?"

"How can we ever find out who we really are?"

I sighed. "I don't know, Shelly. I don't know."

CHAPTER 19

GRAY dormant tree branches silhouetted themselves against a pale gray sky. Gray rain fell on charcoal streets, cold streets, sometimes so cold the charcoal turned white, which was better.

I registered for winter term.

Name: Rebecca A. Lorimer (Adamson)

I signed up for Sidney's drama class. He'd promised me a part in the one-act play they were putting on that term, and he remained true to his word. It was a small part, but it was an angry part, and that was good. I could scream and yell all I wanted and stomp around the stage being obnoxious. It was wonderful.

We had play practice two nights a week, but we often rehearsed during class time as well. Jesse had one of the lead roles.

"She's upstaging me again," Jesse complained to Sidney one afternoon during rehearsal.

"Rebecca," Sidney said, "I do want you to stay in character, but while Jesse's saying his lines, please don't cause so much commotion. You really are distracting from his part."

"Oh, all right." I was playing the maid, and I had been stomping around the back of the set, tossing cushions on the couch and dusting the furniture with such fury I knocked some of the props off the table. I folded my arms and tapped my foot on the floor. "It would help if I had a few more lines, you know."

"I know, I know. But you'll just have to go through the regular steps," he said. He was pacing back and forth as he spoke, I suppose as he imagined a real play producer would do. "If I gave you a lead role, it would go to your head. You'd drive the rest of us crazy." He waved his arm at the rest of the cast to resume rehearsal.

"Crazy is r-right," Jesse muttered. He acted irritated, but I knew that later he would tell me how well I was doing.

"DO you have time for coffee?" Jesse asked, after class.

The question was unnecessary. I always had time for coffee.

"Sure," I said. "Are you ready?"

"Yep." He fastened the snaps on his demin jacket with its furry lining, and pulled the collar close to his neck. He had to tuck his ponytail inside his jacket, and as he turned his head from side to side I watched his tiny gold earring glisten in the lights from the stage.

As we stepped outside I pulled my scarf tighter around my neck and shoved my hands into my pockets. We headed toward the coffee shop. As we walked along our breath formed miniature clouds around our mouths and even our nostrils.

When we came around the corner of Building 5, I saw a couple about fifty feet away, near the door of the coffee shop.

It was Eliot—and Sylvia.

It was inevitable. I knew they had to run into each other from time to time. The campus was too small not to. I'd thought about that when I decided to return to school. What if I ran into Sylvia? How would I feel? What would I do?

The pain of seeing them together was instant and all-encompassing. I could tell they were not actually together, that they had just run into one another and had stopped to say hello. To be civilized. Sylvia would never be uncivilized. But when I saw them my blood ran cold in my veins—colder than the January air, and I could not move. It was the same paralysis I had experienced outside our bedroom door the night of Eliot's birthday party. My feet were fused to the frozen ground, and after taking a few steps Jesse turned to see why I wasn't beside him.

"Come on, Rebecca," he said. "What's the matter with you?"

I stared past him to Eliot and Sylvia and just then Eliot looked up and saw me. Panic replaced my paralysis.

"Rebecca!" Jesse said. "What's the matter? Where are you going?"

I knew Eliot was following me. I had seen the quick surge of his body toward me before I turned away. I was not as civilized as Sylvia. I could not walk up and say hello. I was plagued by the need to run away, like an injured animal, to lick my wounds in private. I hurried toward my car.

I jammed the key in the lock and turned it frantically. I could hear Eliot's steps on the frozen ground, hurrying toward me—almost running, but not wanting to run. Running was not civilized.

"Rebecca, wait," he called. "Wait!" He reached the car just as I was crawling inside. I started to shut the door but he caught it and grabbed me by the arm. "It's not what you think," he said.

"You don't know what I think," I said. I tried to pull away from him. "Let me go."

"I want to talk to you."

"Well, I don't want to talk to you."

I tried to pull away from him again and he looked around, afraid someone might see him abducting his wife. "Scoot over," he said. I didn't move. "Scoot over," he repeated, louder this time. He shoved his body against mine and forced me to the other side of the car seat. He took the car keys from my hand, shut the door, and started the engine.

We were silent as we left the campus parking lot.

He drove out of town, past the sign that said Milford City Limits, and into the country. About a mile from town he pulled off the main highway onto a little-used gravel road. Our gravel road. It ran between two fields, with a shallow ditch running along the left side. To the right there was a small turn-out and a rock marker—a huge boulder. It was a memorial of some sort, but we had never known for what or whom. There was a smooth flat area near the top with four holes, where a plaque had been at one time. But the plaque had long ago disappeared, and now moss crept across the surface. In the past, in the spring of our love, we had leaned against the rock on warm summer evenings and felt the soft, cool moss against our bodies as we visited and kissed. Kissed and kissed—unable to get enough of each other. Eliot had proposed to me there, and it was there, one sultry summer evening, our bodies damp and filled with longing, that I had first told him how I wanted to be the mother of his children. How I longed to hold in my arms a new life that we had made together—a little creature that no other two people could create.

Eliot parked the car next to the boulder and for a few minutes we sat in silence. Then I opened my door and made my way to the rock. I leaned against it, my back to Eliot and the car. I heard Eliot's door open, and the sound of his boots crunching against the frozen grass and earth. He stood beside me, his back to the boulder also, and we stared across the silent, sleeping fields. We were almost back to back, and I was reminded of two surviving warriors, surrounded by enemies, fighting to the finish, back to back.

Eliot ran his hand across the top of the rock, across the crumbling moss. It was winter moss, dry and brittle, not soft as I remembered it.

"You know," he said quietly, "sometimes it seems as if we had more of a marriage before we were married than we do now. A real marriage, I mean. Then we were just two people who loved each other and wanted to spend the rest of our lives together, committed to one another." He rubbed his hand back and forth across the moss and it crumbled beneath his touch. "Now it seems there are all these other things in our relationship—responsibilities, roles, expectations. It's no longer just you and me—it's you and me and our roles. When I became involved with . . ."

I stiffened my neck muscles and folded my arms across my chest.

"I'm sorry, Rebecca. I know it hurts you when I talk about her—but, no, listen. You need to know this. When I became involved with Sylvia it reawakened in me that feeling of what it is to relate to another person—person to person. Sylvia and I had no roles to play. We had no expectations of each other. We were just two people who—two people who cared about each other."

I clenched my teeth together. "Shut up, Eliot. Just shut up." My voice was rising. "I don't have to stand here and listen to you talk about Sylvia."

Eliot grabbed me by the shoulders and forced me to look into his face. Steam puffed from his mouth with each breath. "Rebecca, listen to me. Listen to me. I'm trying to tell you something." His voice softened until it was little more than a whisper. "I'm trying to tell you something important. Please listen."

I stared into his eyes. They were bright with his private light of pain. I looked away and nodded.

"Somewhere along the line, things—just all of a sudden something would say to me, 'It used to be like this with Rebecca.' " Eliot ran his fingers through his hair. "This is hard for me to explain. We didn't have a bad marriage. It was fine. It was OK. But somewhere along the line I quit thinking of you as a person—you were just my wife. Wife." He looked at me, surprised. "I even called you that, didn't I?"

I nodded my head.

"Somehow it took my relationship with Sylvia to see what was missing between you and me."

I turned my back on him, jamming my fists into the pockets of my coat. "Oh, great, I suppose I'm supposed to praise God for your affair. It's done wonders for our marriage!" I paced back and forth across the frozen ground. Eliot came beside me, placed his hands on my elbow, and led me back to our rock. He leaned against it and took my hand in his. The light of pain in his eyes floated and melted and burned into mine until I could see tiny flashes of red.

"Rebecca, what I did with Sylvia was wrong. It was wrong from beginning to end, but it's done—it's over. I love you, Rebecca. I always have. Do you understand? I can't undo what I did. And I'm not trying to justify it. I didn't have to have an affair to learn to relate to you as a person again. There were other ways I could have learned it. There had to have been other ways, better ways, good ways. But I didn't learn it those ways. I learned it this way. The point is, I learned it. I learned it, Rebecca. It was a terrible, ugly way to learn a lesson, but I learned it."

"Like Listerine."

"Listerine?"

"The taste you hate twice a day."

"Come on, Rebecca, be serious."

"I am being serious." My voice rose in a crescendo. "What do you mean, be serious?"

Eliot threw his hands in the air. "I don't know." He turned toward me, his back slightly stooped, his arms outstretched. "I'm trying to tell you something—something really important. It's taken me months to work through this—then when I try to explain it to you you respond with a TV commercial."

I took a deep breath and lifted my chin slightly. "OK," I said, looking at him from beneath lowered eyelids. "Just what is it you're trying to tell me?"

Eliot took my hand in his. "Rebecca, I guess what I've been saying is I want another chance. I'm asking for a chance to start over—to get to know each other again. Not just live together, not just keep a household functioning, but to know each other, love each other."

I slid my tongue across my back molars. I felt something shift. Probably a loose filling. I pressed it with my tongue, and the cold January air touched an exposed nerve.

Eliot continued. "Rebecca, I don't want to lose you. I know it's been hard to forgive me. Can't you try? I know we can make it work. I know we can. Something has gotten lost over the years, but we can find it again." His eyes burned into mine. "We can find it again—I know we can."

I swam into the pain in his eyes, thrashing about in their depths. Maybe we could. Maybe we could somehow find ourselves and find each other and begin to put things back together again. *I know it's hard to forgive me . . . forgive and ye shall be forgiven . . . we were just two people who cared about each other . . . when I became involved . . .*

The piercing pain of a raw nerve.

It was a loose filling for sure. I would have to make an appointment with Dr. Shirring, Monday morning. Robert L. Shirring, D.D.S., Doctor of Dental Surgery, Monday morning, first thing.

I did make an appointment with Dr. Shirring Monday morning. And when I wrote my appointment date on the calendar, a shaft of pain shot through my body. January 20. I was going to the dentist on

Eliot's birthday. January 20—the day I learned about Eliot and Sylvia. Sylvia and Eliot.

The memory ripped through my body like a saber, leaving my nerve endings raw and exposed, pulsing with pain.

What was Eliot talking about—starting over? He didn't know what he was talking about.

CHAPTER

20

I COULD see Alison was taken aback by my attitude, but I continued my story. "You should have seen him," I said, "sitting there all alone in the kitchen eating the pudding he'd worked so hard to fix." I chuckled again, but Alison didn't laugh with me.

"I don't understand how you can laugh at Eliot," she said after an awkward pause. "He's obviously bending over backwards to please you." She leaned forward. "Rebecca, you know how important I think it is for you to be yourself, but . . . well, you can be yourself without destroying Eliot in the process. Eliot is a reasonable man. He's not like some men who really *are* insecure or chauvinistic. Why do you insist on turning your home into a battleground when it's not necessary? What is it doing to the children? Surely you can be yourself without ruining your relationship with Eliot."

I stared at Alison and didn't respond. It was true, I hadn't been thinking about the children much lately. But ruin my relationship with Eliot? There were a few things Alison didn't understand about my relationship with Eliot.

WE were sitting in a tiny coffee shop in Washington Square—a shopper's paradise:

*There's more to compare
At Washington Square.*

Alison had called the week before to say school was taking up too much of my time. She was jealous. I had agreed to go shopping with her. "A typical way for the housewife to pass time," I had chided.

"Oh, brother," she had replied.

Alison took a bite of her Danish pastry and continued her argument. "When we got married Dave and I both had certain expectations—things we agreed upon. Well, I suppose we had some expectations the other didn't know anything about—we all have those—but for the most part, I think we understood each other's expectations. One of those was that Dave would earn the living and I would take care of the home."

"You both expected that because that's what society demands—"

"Just a minute, Rebecca, I wasn't finished. It doesn't make any difference whether we had those expectations because of social pressure or not. The fact remains that we expected them and we were in agreement."

"OK, OK. So what?"

"Well, say I'm pretty content being at home— not working somewhere else—and I am." She gave a loose shrug, as if apologizing for her contentment. "I like my freedom. I have no desire to be tied down to a nine-to-five job."

I stared at her without smiling, waiting for her to continue.

"So one day Dave comes home from work and says he's decided to quit his job. He wants to stay home and take care of the house. He wants me to go get a job. Would that be fair?"

"Well, if you agreed to—"

"No, that's what I'm saying—if I didn't agree to anything, if all of a sudden Dave came home and said, 'I don't want to work anymore. You work. You make the living.' What if I don't want to work? What if I hate working and always hated working and Dave always knew I hated working? Would it be fair for him to come home and suddenly say, 'Well, I know we agreed I would make the living in this family, but I've changed my mind. I'm just not going to do it anymore'?"

"Well . . ."

"Well, what?"

I shook my head. "Well, I just don't think Dave would ever do anything like that."

"Rebecca," Alison's voice was a mixture of impatience and amusement. "I know he wouldn't. I'm saying, if he did, would it be fair? Would it be fair for him to suddenly quit holding his end of the bargain—insist I take on his job?"

"I don't know," I said. "I don't know if it would be fair or not. The thing is, Alison, I don't really care. I don't care if it's fair."

Alison shook her head. "I just don't understand you anymore."

I started to explain myself further, then stopped. I was well into my assertiveness class by then. It was not my responsibility to make people understand me. If they didn't understand me, that was their problem.

"Well, that's how I feel," I said. I shrugged my shoulders and changed the subject. "I'm going to be in a play next month. The drama class is putting on a one-act play."

"What part do you have?"

"The maid. It's just an eensy part, but it's a start. Jesse has the main role."

"Who's this Jesse you keep talking about?"

"Oh, he's really interesting. He's one of the first kids I met when I started school. I thought he was a Hell's Angel. He still laughs about that. He has a slight stutter. But only in real life."

Alison gave me a crooked look.

"I mean, just when he's talking for real—not when he's acting. When he's acting he doesn't stutter at all." I shook my head. "Isn't that funny?" I put a dab more cream in my coffee and stirred it around slowly, watching it marbleize and turn milky brown. I lifted my eyes to meet Alison's and then stared into my coffee again. "I think he's gay," I said. I glanced back at Alison. I could almost read her mind. *What next*, she was saying to herself. *What next?*

"What makes you think so?"

"Well, he wears an earring in one ear . . . and he walks kind of funny."

"Rebecca—"

"Well, Eliot thinks he is, too. In fact Eliot's very adamant about it."

"Does it matter to you?"

"What? What Eliot thinks?"

"No, whether or not Jesse's gay."

"Well, I guess that's what bothers me. It doesn't really. Somehow I feel like it should."

Alison nodded her head.

"I'd just like to know, one way or the other."

"You could always ask him."

"I suppose I could." I paused and took a sip of coffee. "Maybe I don't want to know. Not really."

After we finished our coffee, we shopped for about an hour. Alison needed a new pair of earrings. We stopped at the jewelry counter at Meier and Frank. I rested my elbows on the countertop while Alison tried on first one pair of earrings and then another. She would turn her head from side to side as she studied her reflection in the mirror, pulling her hair back so she could see the earrings. I wondered if Jesse did that, if he pulled his long wavy hair back and turned his head from side to side admiring his earring. Alison finally decided on a silver pair, cube-shaped—a silver box sitting on each of her ear lobes. As soon as she paid for them we began looking for a place to eat lunch. It was obvious our coffee and lunch breaks were more important to us than shopping.

"How about Rian's?" Alison said. "That's supposed to be good."

"That sounds fine," I said.

After we'd eaten, we lingered over yet another cup of coffee. "Do you still have a class on Friday morning?" Alison said.

"Yep."

"Shoot. I miss you at Bible study."

"Are you still going to that?"

"Somebody has to keep them stirred up."

"Is it awful?"

"At times."

"Are they still talking about submission?"

"Sometimes."

"Sick," I said.

"Now, Rebecca," Alison said, wagging her finger at me, "submission is a biblical principle."

"I think that was my line," I said, laughing. "Don't tell me you're switching on me."

"You're the one who's switched," she said. "I'm still here in no-man's-land, looking at everything from every possible angle. But you—well, you've really changed."

"Too much?"

Alison shrugged her shoulders. "A lot."

"You think I'm going off the deep end?"

Alison looked at me solemnly. "I think you're angry about something."

"What if I am?"

She rested her elbows on the table and interlaced her fingers, nestling her chin on her hands. "You won't get anywhere. You'll just keep going in circles. You can take all the assertiveness training you want and do your own thing and have your consciousness raised to high heaven, but if you're angry about something it will all turn back on itself." She hesitated. "You need to deal with the anger."

My eyes felt like coals burning in my head. I was afraid to look away from Alison and afraid to blink. Finally I lowered my head and studied my hands in my lap. *Don't cry.*

I changed the subject again.

"Did you know my grandmother was a feminist?" I said suddenly.

I could see Alison hesitate. She was deciding whether to let me change the subject or whether to press me about my anger. I saw her eyes relax and I knew she had decided to give me my space.

I was grateful.

Having decided to let me off the hook, Alison rested her chin in her hands. "Really?" she said.

CHAPTER 21

THERE were five of us in the car, headed for a Christian women's retreat. It was crowded and I was angry with myself for coming. The scenery along the Sunset Highway toward Cannon Beach passed the window in an unhappy blur, and I couldn't decide who to blame.

Why had I decided to come? Eliot had insisted, I thought. But then, I knew that wasn't true. He had wanted me to come—but he hadn't insisted. Eliot didn't insist on anything—not anymore. I tried to feel victorious about that, as if I'd won the war, but it was hard to feel like the victor. For one thing, Eliot didn't act like the vanquished. He seemed too strong, inside. He no longer threatened to sulk if I didn't live my life according to his plan. It was as if he had won a battle over himself and would not allow me to snatch it from him.

Who was I trying to please then? Alison? Certainly not myself. Please yourself—don't live your life trying to please others. That was my motto. At least, I'd been trying to adopt that motto.

So why was I here? I must have backslidden.

I shook my head and stared at the fields and trees, at the mountains in the distance. Well, no matter. Three days. I could endure it. Then next month I'd do what I wanted to do—what I really wanted to do. I'd go to Ashland with Jesse, Sidney Wolfe, and the others.

When we arrived at the conference center we registered in the foyer of the main hall. I wrote *Rebecca A. Lorimer* on the registration form. I added *Adamson* in parenthesis.

Using my mother's maiden name gave me a peculiar sense of pleasure—of completing something that had remained unfinished.

Right after Daddy died, while cleaning out the attic, Mother and I had come across a box of old feminist pamphlets written by her mother. When I questioned Mother about Grandma Lorimer, she couldn't remember her being a feminist at all. We decided her enthusiasm must have vanished in the same way that whole early movement had disappeared—swallowed up in the seemingly impossible conflict between raising a family and having a career.

But I admired her initial efforts. Some of the things she had written were pretty radical, so it gave me pleasure to use her name—even if it really was her husband's.

After we'd finished registering, we stacked our things in the cramped rooms. We had three hours of free time before dinner, so we headed for the row of shops that lined the main street of Cannon Beach.

The tiny town had developed into a rustic, artsy community, but as we poked around in the shops I realized how long it had been since I'd gone shopping with a bunch of women—and how much my interests had changed. I faked enthusiasm over Calico placemats, patchwork quilts, and eyelet aprons. I admired turquoise earrings, turquoise necklaces, and turquoise watchbands.

Finally we came to a used bookstore. My eyes traveled over the rows of faded books. I smelled the dust in the air and heard it whisper against the soles of my shoes. I winced with the joy of touching native soil.

Within five minutes the rest of the women were ready to move on. I told them I'd meet them back at the campground. Alison argued with me, but finally they left. I spent the rest of the afternoon snooping through the dusty old books. I was aware of my aloneness and felt melancholy—and I was pleased with my melancholy. I bought an old translation of *Madame Bovary*, a small volume of Shakespeare sonnets, and, for reasons I didn't understand, a book about John Winthrop, the first governor of the Massachusetts colony.

I returned to the campground just in time for dinner. Alison apologized for leaving me by myself. I explained that it was fine, that I had enjoyed myself. But she wouldn't believe me. She kept feeling sorry for me and her sympathy put me on edge.

The first evening session was an orientation meeting with lots of announcements. When we returned to our rooms it was like a junior high summer camp. Beds were short-sheeted, nightgowns were stolen, and Marlene began the endless moth joke she told each year.

The Saturday workshop was on how to organize your household. "It's nice for husbands and children to come home to a tranquil, orderly home," the workshop leader said. She promised that with her plan you wouldn't need more than three or four hours a day to take care of household chores. As we left the chapel I felt short-tempered.

"It all sounds complicated and unnecessary," I said.

"Oh, I think it sounds great," Marlene chirped. "I can hardly wait to get home and try it out."

I scowled at her. "Well, I can't imagine spending four hours a day working around the house."

"Really? If I could get my housework down to four hours I'd feel like a new woman."

"Good grief, what do you do? Wax the sidewalks?"

Alison pulled me aside. "It takes a lot of time to bake all that bread," she whispered.

I laughed. It was my first real laugh of the weekend. Marlene glanced back at us suspiciously. "Well, how much time do you spend?" she said.

"I don't know, about half an hour, I guess." I shrugged my shoulders to indicate how unimportant housework was to me.

Marlene was genuinely shocked. "Half an hour! How do you manage that?"

"Have you seen her house lately?" Alison interjected.

I ignored Alison. "The kids do some of it—or Eliot."

Marlene's mouth fell open. *"Eliot?"*

"Sure."

For the first time, I was proud of Eliot and the children—proud of the way they pitched in. Normally I just felt resentful because they still considered it my work—the nagging suggestion that they were merely doing me a favor until I came to my senses.

"Well, that's really . . . nice," said Marlene. Her voice trailed into silence.

WE had fried chicken for dinner—fried chicken, mashed potatoes, and green beans with bits of bacon mixed in. Everyone exclaimed over the green beans, because of the bacon bits, I guess. There was apple crisp for dessert—miniscule squares of apple crisp in mint green Melmac sauce dishes.

The dinner conversation returned to the earlier workshop and I was relieved when it was time for the evening service. It began with songs and announcements, as usual, but the speaker was new, not the one who had conducted the seminars in the afternoon. Her face was narrow and her features plain, but her eyes were alive with the light of intellect and I decided she might be worth listening to.

After a few preliminary remarks, she announced her text. Jeremiah 3. As she read the passage from Jeremiah, the words drifted in and out of my mind, some rooting, others falling by the wayside. *Then the Lord said to me in the days of Josiah the king, "Have you seen what faithless Israel did? She went up on every high hill and under every green tree, and she was a harlot there."*

Adultery.

"For all the adulteries of faithless Israel, I had sent her away and given her a writ of divorce . . ."

Divorce?

"In spite of all this her treacherous sister Judah did not return to Me with all her heart, but rather in deception."

Deception, pretense, a shell of a marriage.

"Faithless Israel has proved herself more righteous than treacherous Judah."

Why? Because Judah pretended to return to God but didn't return with all her heart. The outward form, but not the inner love. The innards ripped away until there was only a shell left. Sleeping with the corpse of a lover.

I wanted to clap my hands over my ears. My head was inside a bell, clanging and clanging. *Leave me alone. Leave me alone.*

People will be lovers of themselves . . . without love, unforgiving . . . having the form of godliness, but denying its power. Without love, unforgiving.

She ended with prayer, and after a moment of silence the women began shuffling about, picking up their purses and stuffing notes into their Bibles. I opened my eyes and was embarrassed to realize I had a hand clapped over each ear. I glanced from side to side hoping no one had noticed.

The women were more subdued than usual, but after a few minutes the air was filled once again with chatter. I was reminded of how the sound of a roomful of women resembled that of a hen yard. It was a comparison that came to my mind frequently at ladies' luncheons and women's Bible studies, and it never failed to bother me. I was irritated because it was true and because I noticed it. But most of all, it irritated me that I was part of it.

It seemed warm and stuffy inside the chapel, and when we stepped outside the fresh air felt wonderful.

"Rebecca?"

"Yes?"

It was Alison. "How about going for a walk on the beach? It's a beautiful evening."

She sounded almost bashful, afraid I would reject the idea—as if rejecting her idea would be rejecting her. And it would be, because the night was beautiful and I loved walking on the beach. And if I said no, it would only be because I didn't want to be with her—or with anyone.

What had Alison ever done to make me reject her? Nothing—except once in awhile make me face myself.

And sometimes she made me laugh.

"OK," I said.

We told the others we would be back later and I held my breath, hoping nobody would decide to come along.

Nobody did.

We walked across the campground in silence and then through the quiet streets of Cannon Beach to the sandy shore. The air was heavy with gritty, salty moisture, and the moon hung tangerine in the deep night sky.

Our shoes sank into the sand and the sand slipped inside them.

"Let's go barefoot."

"I'm wearing pantyhose."

"Oh, me too. Well, let's take them off," Alison giggled.

"Take them off?"

"Sure."

"Can anyone see us?"

"I don't think so."

We hid as best we could behind the logs on the beach as we slipped out of our slacks and removed our pantyhose. We stood on one foot and then the other, laughing at the thought that someone might be watching.

"There," I said. "That's much better." I wiggled my feet in the sand and reveled in the gritty softness between my toes. I stared across the smooth sand to the ocean with its pie-shaped stream of moonlight and quoted softly:

> *Decades of Aprils*
>   *Slip away*
> *And I sit*
>   *On the April soft soil*
> *Waiting for May.*

"What?"

We walked toward the ocean. "It's part of a poem I wrote once. Mother always told me I couldn't go barefoot in a month with an R in it. I never take off my shoes in early spring without wondering if it's really OK. I still feel like I should wait for May."

Alison nodded her head but didn't respond. We walked on in silence. We listened to the pounding of the breakers and the quiet caress of the ocean as it curled across the sand and lapped at our bare feet.

"I brought some matches," Alison said. "Let's build a fire."

It had been years since I'd built a fire on the beach. Even before we lit it I could smell the pungent fumes inside my nostrils.

We gathered driftwood and emptied our pockets of scraps of paper to get it started. It took some doing, but before long the flames were crackling. We sat on a log staring at the hot tongues of fire. The smoke blew in our faces. We moved. It followed us.

"Someone should write their dissertation on that," I said.

"What?"

"Campfire smoke—a study in the habits of."

Alison laughed softly, then fell silent. I continued to stare at the leaping flames. Alison turned to me suddenly. "You were upset tonight. How come?"

"I wasn't upset."

"You had your hands clapped over your ears during prayer."

"You were supposed to have your eyes closed."

"You made up for me—you had both your ears and eyes closed."

I picked up a stick and poked it into the fire. There was a snapping sound and tiny sparks shot through the deep night air. I turned to Alison. Her face was burnished copper and the shadows from the fire played across it, sometimes distorting it into ugliness and other times tracing upon it a mysterious beauty. I supposed my face looked strange to her too—part demon, part saint.

"How important is it to obey God?" I said.

She paused a moment and the shadows from the fire stained her cheeks with spectral beauty. "I suspect it's very important."

I lifted my chin and gazed toward the murmuring ocean. "Alison, have you . . . have you ever had to obey God on something really important—do something you really didn't want to do?"

Alison stared into the fire. She was more thoughtful than usual, slower to respond. Finally she said, "How old were you when you commited your life to God?"

"Oh, I don't know, about six or seven."

Alison nodded her head. "I was nineteen," she said. She turned to face me and the unfamiliar pathos in her eyes looked stranger still because of the coppery shadows playing across her face. "I was engaged to be married," she said, staring into the frantic flames of our bonfire. Her face was drawn and sober. "Paul wasn't a Christian. At first I thought he would change. I told him all about God and about Jesus coming to earth to reconcile mankind to himself. All of it. But he wasn't interested. Finally he told me he didn't want me talking about it anymore."

Alison touched the tip of the stick on the sand and circled it in a futile gesture. Her voice was plaintive. "Not talk about God? He was the breath of life to me." She lifted her eyes and looked into my face. "I knew a future with Paul would become meaningless. I had to break up with him." Her eyes were filled with the old pain. "I loved him," she said. "I loved him very, very much." She moved the stick in a circle, round and round. Instead of getting deeper, the track remained the same. As soon as the stick passed by the dry sand fell back into place.

Her voice was quiet. "If I had chosen my way instead of God's way I would have spent the minutes, hours, even years of my life in disobedience. When I chose God instead of Paul, I forfeited the days and hours of my life with Paul to God. They were a part of my life I wanted to live, but didn't."

Alison let the stick drop to the sand and she rested her chin in her hands, her elbows on her knees. She stared into the fire and she seemed so far away I was surprised when she spoke. "Sometimes it seems the deepest longings of our hearts would be satisified in disobedience, but I don't think that's ever true. To find our way back to God, the thing we covet must die. Eventually it must die. But the death is dreadful—a tearing and ripping away of the thing coveted."

I watched Alison as she spoke. She spoke quietly, and not to me, really, more to herself. "Tearing, ripping, writhing in anguish. Always the death has to come, and after the death, grief, and after the grief—the void." Her words had fallen into a whisper and when she finished we stared into the fire with only the soft snapping of the flames and the pounding of the ocean waves to disturb the quiet.

"Is obedience always that difficult?" I asked. My voice was so soft I thought perhaps the sound of the waves had carried my words away. But after a moment Alison responded.

"I don't know." She turned her face toward mine. "But sometimes it is." After a moment she said, "Why did you ask?"

I lowered my eyes. "I was just thinking about something."

"What?"

"Well . . . forgiveness, I guess."

"Forgiveness?"

"I was wondering . . . I was wondering if not forgiving someone is being disobedient to God."

Alison was thoughtful a moment. "I hadn't really thought of it that way, but I suppose it is." She ran her fingers through her hair. "Jesus said that if someone sins against us and repents—even seven times in one day—we must forgive him." She shook her head. "I guess that's pretty clear."

"*Must* forgive him? Does it say *must* forgive?"

Alison nodded her head. She swirled the stick on the sand again. Doodling.

Jesus writing in the dust with his fingertip. *Neither do I condemn you. Go and sin no more.*

I stared into the fire.

Alison leaned forward. Her face was beautiful and serious. "Do you need to forgive someone?" she said quietly.

I bit my lower lip and stared into the fire. I nodded my head ever so slightly. I could feel my eyes starting to burn and I blinked them rapidly.

"Rebecca, what is it?" Alison said. "Please, tell me."

I leaned forward and rested my chin in my hands, my lips pressed against my tightly curled fingertips. I relaxed the rigidness of my back and leaned forward, allowing my back to curve round in a slight hunch. I knew I needed to talk to someone. But I wasn't sure how to begin. How do you talk about something like that? I took a deep breath.

"Remember the night of Eliot's birthday party?" I said.

Alison nodded her head.

"Do you remember when I asked you to pour coffee for me, while I ran upstairs?"

Alison waved her hand through the air. "Well, not really, but go ahead."

"I followed Eliot up there because he was looking for some photographs and I had moved them." Alison nodded her head. "But when I got to the top of the stairs I noticed he was in our bedroom—talking on the telephone." I paused and stared into the fire. After a few minutes I lifted my eyes and looked into the distance, toward the sound of the ocean. "He was talking to Sylvia," I said. "Sylvia Weston. I heard him tell her that he loved her." I glanced back at Alison. "They were having an affair, Alison. Sylvia and Eliot were having an affair."

Alison leaned forward and gripped my fingers. She closed her eyes and squeezed her eyelids together. "Oh, Rebecca," she said. "I'm sorry. I had no idea." She shook her head and looked into my eyes. Her eyes were gentle and filled with compassion.

My eyes filled with tears and I wiped them with my sleeve. "They broke it off," I said. "As soon as I found out, they broke it off, but . . ." I shrugged my shoulders.

"Are you sure?" she said. "I mean do you sometimes wonder if maybe . . ."

I shook my head. I had seen the look on Eliot's face when he told me it was over. If he said it was over, it was over. You don't manufacture that kind of pain. "I'm sure," I said.

"But . . . ," Alison said, "you can't forgive him?"

I shook my head. "Alison, how do you go about forgiving something like that?"

She shook her head. "I don't know. I don't know what I'd do in your shoes." She sat very still as the coppery shadows of the fire played across her face. "But I can see your anger is affecting you, Rebecca, changing you into something I'm not sure you want to become. You're really only making it harder on yourself."

I shrugged my shoulders.

Alison was silent for a moment as she looked into my face. "You don't have to forgive him," she said. "Nobody can make you forgive him. You can live the rest of your life filled with anger and resentment if that's what you want. But Rebecca," she said with soft intensity, "if you want more than that, you might as well get on with it. There's no sense hanging on to that anger any longer than you have to. It's not worth it."

I stared at Alison. I didn't know whether to feel angry or grateful or hurt or misunderstood.

"It just doesn't seem fair," I said.

"It's not," she replied.

CHAPTER 22

"WELL, how was the retreat?" Eliot asked when I got home.

"Fine."

"Fine? That's all? Just fine?"

He had wanted me to come home reformed. I tossed my handbag on the bed and plopped down beside it. "Fine," I repeated, lifting my arms and letting them drop. I kicked off my shoes. "It was fine." I shrugged my shoulders. For the first time in months I wanted to give Eliot what he wanted. He had hoped I'd come home from the retreat repentant and humble, ready to turn over a new leaf. He wanted his old wife back, the one who wanted to please him—even if it sometimes meant pretending to be something she wasn't.

But I was still pretending—pretending to be married, pretending I was part of a relationship, pretending in front of our relatives and friends, pretending before our own children. I stared at Eliot and felt the old conflict inside myself—the desire to do what was expected of me. Retreats were places for revival, renewal. One part of me gloated at having survived the weekend unscathed—unrevived. The other part felt it was necessary to make an excuse.

"The food was lousy," I said.

Eliot studied my face and his shoulders sagged. "I'm surprised," he said. "It's usually pretty good."

"It was lousy," I repeated.

That was the end of our conversation.

MAYBE I was trying to make up for surviving the retreat unrevived when I decided to have Easter dinner at our house—labor for my atonement. Usually we went to Mother's.

"I think I'll fix Easter dinner this year," I said to Eliot one evening.

"That would be nice."

"That way," I continued, "we could invite Alison and Dave. They don't have any family around here. Did you know they sent Mother a sympathy card? I thought that was really thoughtful."

"A sympathy card? Oh, you mean when your dad died. Yes, that was thoughtful."

"And Lance and Susan, of course."

"Uh-huh."

I counted on my fingers—that would be twelve, a nice even number. We would all fit around one table. I hated having to worry about two tables.

"When's Easter?" Eliot asked.

"Three weeks, I think."

"Three weeks." Eliot was thoughtful.

"Why?"

"Huh? Oh, I was just thinking about the bathroom. It would be nice if I could get the bathroom finished before then."

Get the bathroom finished? I hadn't even thought about the bathroom. "That would be nice," I said.

Eliot began working on the bathroom the next day after school. The supplies he had bought the summer before were sitting in the garage in dusty boxes—new light fixtures, floor tile, Sheetrock, and even a new mirror. Every afternoon Eliot hurried home after school and worked on the bathroom until after dark.

"ELIOT, are you going to eat dinner?" I called, one evening.

No answer.

"Are you going to eat dinner?" I hollered again. I knew he couldn't hear me. He hadn't even stopped hammering. I set the salad on the table and walked to the bathroom, stopping in the doorway.

"Eliot."

"Huh?" His back was to me. He was pounding narrow silver nails into the Sheetrock.

"Are you going to eat dinner?"

Eliot flexed his arm and slipped the hammer neatly into the loop on his overalls in a motion both smooth and impressive, like a gunslinger returning his pistol to his holster after a successful shoot-out. He turned around and the nails he held between his teeth glittered like five silver fangs. "Idthinshio," he said. He took the nails from his mouth. "I don't think so." He turned back to the wall. "Maybe you could keep it warm for me." He put the nails back between his teeth and removed the hammer from its holster. He glanced back at me, silver fangs gleaming.

"OK," I said.

I put a plate of food in the oven for Eliot. After the rest of us had eaten and the kitchen was cleaned up, I stood with my elbows on the countertop and stared out the kitchen window. It was still early evening, but I could see my own reflection in the window and, behind me, the door that led down the hall toward the bathroom and the noise of Eliot's hammer. The sound carried me back to an earlier time—to the first home we owned, on Ellendale Lane. I remembered showing it to my father.

"Eliot's going to knock out this wall," I had said, motioning toward the wall that separated the dining room from the cramped kitchen. "That way the kitchen won't be so dark."

As I had led him through the bare rooms I had sensed his disapproval. But he didn't say anything. Mother had talked to him. I led him into the living room. The paint on the walls was dull and chipped. There were patches where the beige paint was peeling away, exposing the room's history. It had been blue once, green another time. I chipped at the peeling paint with my fingernail. "I can't believe it," I said. "Purple. Who in their right mind would paint a room purple?" My shoulders tensed instinctively. Eliot, my father would say—Eliot.

But he didn't say it.

"We're going to repaint in here," I said. "And put down a new carpet."

"Is Eliot going to do it himself?" Dad asked, breaking his self-imposed silence.

"Yes," I said. "It's much too expensive to have it done."

Dad nodded his head but didn't reply.

He didn't believe Eliot would do it, not for a long time anyway, five years maybe—five years of living with a ragged carpet and chipped paint.

I didn't believe Eliot would do it either.

Dad had rubbed the sole of his shoe back and forth across the thin carpet. His eyes wandered along the baseboard, taking in the paint slopped onto the edge of the carpet by a careless painter. His eyes rested on a crack in the plaster. He was biting his tongue, trying to hold back his criticism.

I shouldn't have gone to Mother. I should have talked to him myself. But I couldn't. I wanted to, but the words just wouldn't come out.

Mom had drawn it out of me. "What's wrong?" she'd said.

There was no sense trying to sidestep her. She always knew when something was bothering me. "It's Dad," I'd said.

Dad put his hands on his hips and let his eyes roam along the top of the walls, checking for structural defects. "Well," he said, "it isn't much, is it?" A small burst of air followed his words, as if he couldn't hold in his disapproval any more than he could hold excess air in his lungs.

I had lifted my chin. "It will be fine," I said. "When we get it fixed up, it will be fine."

"Dad," Eliot had called from the basement, "come down here. I want you to see the workshop."

Dad glanced at me. "Go ahead," I said. "I'm going out back."

I had closed the back door behind myself with a sigh. I had to push in and down on the doorknob so the door would shut. "That's no big thing," Eliot had said, when I told him the door didn't shut right. "I'll just take the rasp to it. It will be fine."

But when? When would he take the rasp to it?

I made my way through the unkempt backyard to the stream that wound its way across the back of the property. I could hear the gurgling water before I could see it. The sound alone caused some of the tension to drain from my body. I pushed aside the tall grass and a tiny gasp escaped my lips as I stared into the clear blue-green water. A fish. There was actually a fish in our creek. It weaved its way upstream, its silver body undulating in the cool water. Below the fish I could see through the water to the pebbles of the creek bed. Shafts of sunlight streamed through the water onto the rocks—like beams of logic sometimes pierce the mind.

I fell to my knees beside the stream. This was why we had bought the house. I loved the stream. And Eliot knew it.

I heard a rustle in the grass behind me. Dad pushed his way through the weeds and sat down next to me. His eyes met mine and I was startled by their blueness, by their clarity.

He pulled some grass from the damp soil and tossed it into the creek, watching the water carry it downstream. "Mom told me about your talk," he said. I lowered my head and nodded without speaking. He continued. "I wish you could have come to me."

"I do too," I whispered.

I had wrapped my arms around my legs and rested my chin on my knees. "He's my husband," I said. I stared into the water. "Every time you criticize him—every time I listen to you criticize him, I feel like I've betrayed him—been unfaithful." Tears formed in my eyes and I blinked in irritation.

He pulled out a clump of grass, roots and all, and tossed it into the stream. It muddied the stream temporarily. He stared into the water thoughtfully. "I guess you see something in him I don't see," he said. Then he turned his head sharply and looked at me. I looked into his face. "But if you see it," he said, "I believe it's there. If you see it, it's there."

I had nodded my head.

Dad had cleared his throat. "That's quite a workshop Eliot has down there," he said. "With a workshop like that he just might get the house fixed up in a jiffy." He had looked back into the creek. The mud had washed away and the water was running clear again.

"I know," I had replied. "He might."

NOW, as I listened to the *tap, tap* of Eliot's hammer, I was filled with the same hope and despair. *He might get it done*, I thought. *He might*.

"Knock, knock."

It was Matthew. He leaned his sturdy body against the counter next to mine and folded his grimy arms on the countertop.

"Who's there?"

"Dwayne."

"Dwayne who?"

"Dwayne the bathtub—I'm dwowning."

"Cute," I said. I never knew how to respond to knock-knock jokes. I should have groaned. Groaning was better. I focused on Matthew's dirty arms. "Did you take a bath today?"

Matthew thought a moment. "Is one missing?"

I stared at him. He'd been reading his joke book again.

For the first time in a long while, I really looked at Matthew. I took in the clumsy knot in his broken shoelace, his football jersey, half in, half out, and his hair standing up in all the wrong places. I wondered how it felt to live inside a ten-year-old boy body. He had come beside me in the gathering darkness of a lonely spring evening and shared his jokes with me—a part of his world, a part of himself. Suddenly I was afraid he would stop. I was afraid that without warning he would recognize my indifference to the part of his world he was sharing with me and stop.

I rumpled his thick brown hair with my hand. "Yes," I said, "there is a bath missing. And if I ever find out you had anything to do with it—" I glared at him in mock threat.

He held up his dirty arms, like a teller during a bank robbery. "I didn't, honest! I didn't take it." He dropped his arms and shoulders in pretend despair. "Well, I guess if somebody took the bath then I can't take one tonight, huh?"

"I guess not," I said, shaking my head in dejection. "Not till we find it. But you'd better wash your arms before you go to bed—they're pretty bad."

"OK."

He left the kitchen and I turned once again to the window, staring into the gathering darkness. They were growing up too fast, all of them. Sometimes I felt like I hardly knew them anymore.

"Mom?" It was Matthew again.

"Hmm?"

"I love you." His face was contorted with the embarrassed shyness of a ten-year-old who was stepping out of character for a moment. He gave me an awkward hug and looked up at me. He wanted to kiss me, but didn't know how. I leaned down and he kissed me on the cheek.

"I love you too, Matthew," I said, squeezing his tough body against mine.

"Mom?"

"Hm-hmm?"

"I haven't slept for days."

"How come?"

Maternal concern. A warped psyche? Inadequate mothering?

"I only sleep at night." Grin.

I put my hands on my hips. "Matthew," I said, "go to bed."

"OK. 'Night, Mom."

"Good night, Matthew."

CHAPTER 23

PERHAPS because I'd spent so little time cooking in recent months, the family Easter dinner loomed before me as a giant undertaking. What should I serve? Ham? I supposed so, and scalloped potatoes.

Eliot got the bathroom finished just in time. Wallpaper Wonders called the Wednesday before to say the paper was in. Eliot put it up Thursday evening. I bought a giant pink geranium and planted it in the pickle crock I'd kept squirreled away in the basement for the occasion.

The alarm rang early Easter morning, and before I got out of bed I studied the sky through the bedroom window. Resurrection morning. Strange that the sky was draped in clouds like the gray satin folds of a coffin lining.

As I put the extra leaves in the dining room table, I wondered for the hundredth time whether twelve people would make it too crowded. Over the years we had often had that many at our table, but I never set it for twelve without wondering if it would be too cramped. I put the ham in the oven and peeled the potatoes.

By the time we left for church I felt like dinner was pretty well under control. We were only a few minutes late for Sunday school and I slipped into the chair next to Marlene. Eliot slithered in beside me, trying not to make a commotion.

"We're starting a new study today," Marlene whispered. "Hebrews."

"Hmm," I said. Lately it hadn't mattered to me what we studied.

"There's been a lot of controversy over who wrote the Book of Hebrews," Tom began. "Paul is the writer suggested most often. Do any of you know some other possible authors?"

"Apollos?"

"That's possible."

"Barnabas?"

"Another possibility. If it wasn't written by Paul it was almost certainly written by someone well acquainted with him. The christological argument is like Paul's. What are some other possibilities?"

"Priscilla?" I ventured.

"Priscilla?" Tom repeated. He laughed. That's all. He just laughed.

"What's so funny?" I said. "Priscilla was well acquainted with Paul. She was obviously intelligent—she helped instruct Apollos."

Tom shook his head. "The Bible was written by men, Rebecca, not women."

"Who says?" I said.

"Honestly, Rebecca," Marlene interjected. "Sometimes I think you're going off the deep end. You sound like one of those women's libbers or something."

"Maybe I am!" I shot back.

"Well, you'd better make up your mind," she said, heatedly. "You can't be a Christian and a women's libber both."

I stared at her, appalled. "That's strange," I said, my voice calm and deliberate. "I always thought Jesus was one of the first people to stand up for women."

Marlene frowned, and Tom, thoroughly embarrassed, proceeded with the lesson.

I went into a sulk. I refused to listen to the rest of the lesson. I crossed my legs and watched the toe of my shoe swing up and down, up and down.

After Tom finished the lesson there was a short prayer time. "Are there any special requests?" he said. "How about answered prayers? Sometimes we forget to thank God when he answers our prayers."

Marlene raised her hand and explained how she had taken her

elderly mother shopping and had prayed for a good parking spot and God had provided one right in front of Penney's. I thought I'd be sick. I knew if I heard one more story about God providing someone with a parking place I was going to flip out. A parking lot attendant—is that all God was—a parking lot attendant? I felt angry with Marlene and every person in that Sunday school class who was nodding his head in acknowledgment. "Yes, isn't it wonderful how God takes care of us." Marlene's parking-lot-praise just added fuel to my disgust of Tom's male Bible. By the time the class was over my stomach was churning and my head was spinning in semi-controlled fury.

As we took our places for the Easter worship service, I put my mind into neutral. I let the organ music pour over my passive mind. Better not listen, just coast, no use getting upset about things.

But when the pastor stood to give the morning message, I automatically turned to the text in my Bible, John 10.

I am the good shepherd; and I know My own, and My own know me, even as the Father knows Me and I know the Father; and I lay down My life for the sheep.

The gospel words dropped from the lips of the pastor and into my heart, but I didn't know what to do with them when they landed.

He calls his own sheep by name and leads them out.

Calls them by name? Which name? Becky, Rebecca, wife, honey, Rebecca Anne Carter, Rebecca Adamson, Becca, Rebecca A. Lorimer?

Did God know who I was?

I tuned out again. Before I knew it the service was over.

IT WAS cramped with twelve at the table. As soon as we sat down I remembered how it had been the last time. We sat like hens on a chicken roost, our wings tucked carefully at our sides.

I watched the platters of food limp around the table with the growing dread that I hadn't fixed enough scalloped potatoes. There was plenty of ham, but the potatoes . . .

"How do you like the bathroom, Susan?" Eliot asked.

Nobody had commented on it.

"I love it," she said. "I couldn't believe you finished it. And that wallpaper—did you pick that out, Eliot?"

"Nope. The wallpaper was Rebecca's department."

Too bad, I thought. Eliot had spent months working on the bathroom and the only thing Susan noticed was my wallpaper—one afternoon in Wallpaper Wonders, drinking coffee. Too bad.

"You should have been in Sunday school this morning, Alison," I said. Dave and Alison attended a church across town. "Tom did it again."

"What?"

"Oh, he makes me so mad. He's such a male chauvinist." I jabbed my fork into a tender pink slice of ham.

"What'd he say?"

"We're studying Hebrews. I suggested Priscilla might have been the writer. Tom laughed. He just laughed."

Dave chuckled. "Well, it is kind of funny. Priscilla? I've never heard of such a thing."

Alison looked at Dave sideways, and Eliot glanced at him as if trying to catch his eye. "Rebecca has had her consciousness raised, Dave," Eliot said, warning him to back off.

"Some Bible scholars make quite a case for it," I said, ignoring Eliot.

Dave took a drink of water. "It just seems unlikely to me," he said. "All the known writers of the Bible were male. Why should all of a sudden a woman writer be—"

"All of a sudden!" I said, louder than I had intended. "You call thousands of years all of a sudden? About time, I would say."

"But Rebecca," Mother said, using her soothing tone, "the Apostle Paul says that women shouldn't teach in the church. I can't imagine a woman writing part of the Holy Bible."

"That Paul has caused more trouble!" I said. "I just can't believe God intended women to be second-class—"

Lance interrupted, "Rebecca, I don't think anybody's talking about second-class citizens. When the Bible talks about women being in subjection—"

"Subjection!" I said, raising the volume a notch again. "Anytime you start talking subjection, I think you really mean inferiority." There were objections all around the table, but I raised my hand and spoke louder to drown them out. "For centuries white men pulled verses out of context to prove that black people were meant to be in subjection to whites. Do you think those slave owners felt guilty about owning slaves? Of course not. They thought they were carrying out God's will. Well, I can't buy the idea that half the human race is supposed to be in subjection to the other half any more than I can believe blacks were supposed to be in subjection to whites." Everyone was silent. "It was that way, but I don't think it was supposed to be that way." I jabbed my fork into another piece of ham. "I'm just tired of watching women be exploited."

"Exploited! Who's exploiting you?" Dave said.

"Everyone." I said. "Women are being exploited everywhere."

Dave smiled and shook his head. His smug face made me furious. "OK," I said, "I'll show you." I pushed back my chair and walked into the kitchen. I returned with a bottle of dishwashing detergent shaped like an hourglass. "Does this remind you of anything?" I said. I was acting a little wild and our dinner guests were getting uncomfortable. They were shifting in their chairs and clearing their throats.

"A bottle of detergent," Lance said.

"Can't you see?" I said. "Can't you? It's shaped like a female body."

"Rebecca," my mother said, using the tone she'd used with me as a child, "that's silly."

"Silly," I said. "It sells detergent, that's what. Don't ask me why women—"

Mother was shaking her head in reproof. "Mother," I said, "why do you think the little old ladies at church bazaars make aprons to fit detergent bottles?" I paused dramatically because I knew mother's bottle of dishwashing soap wore an apron. "They know."

That stopped her. "You don't suppose—," she said, and covered her mouth to hide a giggle.

"That's not all," I said, plopping the bottle of detergent on the dinner table with a thump. "Last week I got a free sample of—"

"Rebecca!" Eliot's face turned red and he glanced around the room. "That's enough."

"What?" Alison said. I could tell her mind was spinning with curiosity.

"I'll go get it and show you," I said, starting to push back my chair again.

"Rebecca!" Eliot said. "That's enough. I mean it."

I hesitated. He meant it. I glanced at the children. Shelly was watching me, amazement spread across her face like a coat of paint. Perhaps I had gone far enough. I settled back in my chair. "Well," I said, "are we ready for dessert?"

I served the pie and coffee and returned to my chair.

"How's your drama class going?" Alison said.

"Great. We're going down to Ashland in a few weeks."

"Ashland?" Eliot said. "I didn't know you were going to Ashland."

"Yep. We're going to the Shakespearean Festival."

"Are you in Wolfe's class?" Dave said, glancing at Eliot.

I nodded.

"Isn't he a little—" He tipped his hand from side to side.

"A little," I said.

"Ashland?" Eliot said again.

BY THE end of the day I had managed to alienate just about everyone. At first they treated me lightly, like they would have a hyperactive child who was sure to settle down as soon as the sugar worked its way out of her system. But as the day wore on and I became more and more belligerent, even Alison became impatient.

"Rebecca, I simply can't believe you want to change your name. You can't be serious."

"Well, I am," I said.

"Change your name?" Mother said, as she entered the kitchen. She waved her hand toward the bathroom. "The bathroom's beautiful, Rebecca. What do you mean change your name? Are you going to go by Becky? Your father would have liked that." Mother was like a little bird, chirping around, trying to keep up with everything.

"No, she wants to change her last name," Susan said with disgust.

"Your last name? Why, whatever for?" She was horrified. "You don't mean *legally* change your name?"

"Yes, legally."

"What in the world would you change it to?"

"Lorimer," I said.

"Lorimer?" The expression on Mother's face was comic. She was surprised, disgusted, and pleased—just as I would have been if Shelly had actually decided to call herself Shelly Carter. I knew Mother couldn't resist a feeling of pride. "Why, that's my maiden name," she said. "Why in the world—?"

"Grandma Lorimer," I said. "The feminist. It's the least I can do to carry on the fight she gave up."

"Oh, Rebecca, I think my mother was very young when she got mixed up with those feminists. She wasn't that way at all. I'm not sure she would want you carrying on for her—not in that way, at least." She shook her head. "She always told me that a home and family were what were really important." She shook her head again. "She always told me that, again and again."

"Trying to convince herself," I muttered. "I think Grandma Lorimer got schnooked."

"Rebecca, don't you talk about my mother that way."

Mother was getting upset. That made Susan upset. "Rebecca—honestly!"

AFTER everyone had left, Eliot followed me into the kitchen with a handful of dirty dishes. "What's this about Ashland?" he said.

"The drama class is going," I said. "Next month."

"Why didn't you tell me?"

"I did."

"I mean before. I felt like an idot at the dinner table—not knowing anything about it. How long have you been planning on going?"

"A month or two."

"Who else is going?"

"The whole class, I guess. Sidney and Jesse for sure."

"Sidney and Jesse? Any other women?"

"You mean besides Jesse?"

"I mean besides you."

"I suppose so. I don't know."

"But you know Sidney and Jesse are going."

"Well, yes. They're my friends, Eliot."

"They're weird."

"They are not."

"Rebecca, that Jesse is as queer as a—" He waved his hand through the air and couldn't think of anything queer. "Well, he's just queer, that's all."

For some reason my thoughts turned to the harems of ancient Persia. I thought of King Xerxes and Queen Vashti, of court officials and eager-to-please personal attendants.

"Well," I said. "I always wanted my own eunuch."

"There's a difference between a eunuch and a homosexual, Rebecca. I can't believe you."

I didn't reply.

"And Wolfe. Everybody on campus knows about him. He'd flip you into bed the first chance he got and walk away without turning back."

"You're a fine one to talk about flipping people into bed, Eliot Adamson."

"Rebecca—"

"Don't 'Rebecca' me," I said. "You've had your fling, Eliot, now you can just let me have mine!"

Eliot paced around the kitchen. "Is that it? Are you getting revenge?"

I flushed with anger. "No, I'm not getting revenge. I'm just doing what I want to do. Why can't you just let me do what I want?"

"Because I love you and I see you heading for trouble. I would like to keep you from getting hurt."

I turned on the water faucet with an angry yank. I stood before Eliot, my hands on my hips, while the water ran furiously into the sink. "Baloney. You reformed people are all alike. I can't stand any of you. When you wanted to mess around you messed around!" I began pacing around the kitchen, stopping for a moment to turn the water back off again. "But, now, oh, now it's all different. You come purring around about being careful and not getting into trouble. You did your thing, Eliot, and I'm going to do mine." I stopped in front of him and looked into his eyes with a stony stare. "Do you hear me, Eliot? I'm going to do mine."

That night, when Eliot and I went to bed, it was late and we were both tired—and still angry. But yet, just before we drifted into sleep, we came together in a silent, grasping—almost unconscious—attempt to unite ourselves. For some reason I remembered the night long before when Eliot had seduced me while secretly wearing his black socks. We had choked with laughter because it was all such fun. But now, as we lay spent in the tangled sheets, I held his head close to mine and whispered, "I need you, I need you," again and again. I clung to him and sobbed.

He stroked my head and said, "I know, I know. It's all right. It's all right to need me." I fell asleep in his arms.

But when I woke in the morning I was furious with myself. I vowed I would not become that vulnerable to him again.

CHAPTER 24

I HAD an unusual dream that night. I didn't dwell on it, but whenever it popped into my mind I shook my head—it had been bizarre, really bizarre.

When I went shopping later in the week for my trip to Ashland, I stopped at Jackson's Bookstore. As I was browsing I came across a dream dictionary and I leafed through it. It said things like, "This is a good omen having to do with finances"—that sort of thing. It reminded me of the horoscope in the newspaper—seemingly harmless tidbits that could be twisted to fit any situation.

I shrugged my shoulders and tried to find the subject of my Easter night dream. *Andiron?* I had been poking people with an andiron. Nothing there. Try *ashes*. First I had rubbed the andiron through the ashes in the fireplace. Back and forth, back and forth. Then I had gone around the room poking people. Not once or twice, but again and again, until they finally cried out in pain or moved away. Nothing there either. *Poking, stabbing, jabbing?* There it was, *jabbing*. It was a family reunion of some sort, in Canada, or Kansas. And my father was there, my dead father, except he was alive. But he was just on leave. We all knew he was really dead and couldn't stay. I even poked at him, jabbed and jabbed at him as he sat all bent and crooked in a rocking chair. Finally he disappeared, just disappeared. Everyone said it was my fault, that he could have stayed longer if I hadn't kept poking him.

> *Jabbing:* If others are jabbing at you it means you aren't living to your fullest potential. If you are poking others it suggests over-aggression. Seeing a psychiatrist might help you work out your aggressiveness.

I laughed to myself and then frowned. A psychiatrist! I slammed the book shut and tossed it back on the rack. I didn't bother to get it in the right slot.

I'd never believed in horoscopes either.

FOR some reason the trip to Ashland really set Eliot off. He couldn't cope.

"I don't like it, Rebecca. I just don't like it. Where are you staying?"

"In a motel."

With whom? That's what he wanted to ask. But he didn't. He ran his fingers through his hair. "If it was a different group of people it would be another matter, but that drama bunch—well, they're just weird, that's all." He straightened his back. "I can't let you do it. I just can't let you go. You will not go to Ashland with a bunch of weirdos. I forbid it."

I stared at Eliot. He forbid it? What did he mean forbid it? He couldn't forbid anything.

"I'm going," I said.

"No, you're not."

"Yes, I am."

"No, you're not."

THE morning we left I woke early. Restless. The cold northern light filtered dimly through the sheer bedroom curtains. By the time the light reached the curtains it had already been filtered through the haze that hung over Milford in the morning hours, and then filtered again through the leaves of the maple tree outside the window.

"I'm trying to protect you, that's all."
"I don't need your protection."
"I think you do."
"Well, I think I don't."

WE met in the campus parking lot, stumbling around in early morning confusion, some of us with pillows in our arms, trying to decide who was going to ride in which car. I ended up in Sidney's Volkswagen with Sidney, Jesse, and Sally. Sally and I had both tried out for the maid's part in the play we'd done winter term. I always imagined she'd begrudged me the role.

As we started down the freeway I scrunched my pillow into the corner and nestled my head into the softness, hoping to catch up some sleep. But I couldn't sleep. As the miles between Milford and Sidney's humming little bug increased I felt a strangeness envelope me.

Weirdos, Eliot had said. They're a bunch of weirdos. *They're not weird,* I thought. But for the first time they did seem like strangers. Sally sat beside me, neither friendly nor unfriendly, but with an indefinable air of resentment. Sidney, behind the wheel, chattered continuously. His conversation was sprinkled with obscenities and never got below the surface. We had come close to knowing each other that night at Bower's Tower, but, although we had become friends, the closeness of that evening had never been repeated, and I had finally come to realize it never would.

Even Jesse seemed strange to me. In the classroom and at the campus coffee shop I had grown accustomed to his ponytail, ragged denims, and boots. But here in a battered Volkswagen, racing down the freeway, farther and farther from home, I saw him through the same eyes I had the first day we met.

He looked like Charles Manson.

WE went to a play that evening and afterwards to a beer garden. But everyone was tired and anxious to rest for the next day. Sally and I were assigned to the same room. Sidney and Jesse were staying in the same motel, two rooms over. Sally and I managed to get ready for bed without exchanging more than ten words.

The next morning the four of us met for breakfast, and as I studied the menu I listened to what was developing between Sidney and Sally.

"Friday Fantasy," Sidney said. He was reading the menu. "Our own special pancake, filled with fruit and topped with a mountain of whipped cream."

"Friday Fantasy?" Sally said, smirking.

Sidney leaned toward her, his elbows on the table. "I had a few Friday fantasies of my own," he said, arching one eyebrow and moving his face even closer to hers. "How about you?"

"Maybe," she said, with a baby pout.

"I'll tell you mine if you'll tell me yours," Sidney said.

Sally giggled. "Maybe later."

I glanced at Jesse. He was studying his menu with more concentration than it merited.

In the morning we toured the theaters and in the afternoon we went shopping. We noticed shades of Shakespeare everywhere. On Main Street we passed the Mark Antony Hotel and the Jester's Gallery. Later we wandered through Lithia Park and on our way to a little wine and cheese shop we descended Shakespeare stairs.

There was a poster in a window announcing a lecture near the Southern Oregon campus—on Siskiyou Boulevard. "Who was Siskiyou?" I said. I thought maybe he was a character in one of Shakespeare's plays.

Sidney smiled a condescending smile. "The Siskiyous are those mountains over there," he said, pointing to the green and purple peaks surrounding us.

"Oh," I said. I shrugged my shoulders. "Well, I thought maybe Siskiyou was a friend of Rosencrantz and Guildenstern." Sidney shook his head and smiled. For good measure I added, "Maybe Siskiyou was an Indian."

"Maybe he was just a mountain, Rebecca. Maybe he was just a mountain."

"No imagination," I retorted.

AS we browsed through the cheese shop and then through a store specializing in stained glass, Sidney and Sally continued their little game of hide-and-seek. Suggest—resist. Imply—demur. Why didn't they just get on with it?

We finally came to a used bookstore, and I sighed in relief. The gift shops had gotten tiresome, and I had wearied of Jesse's running narration on the evils of capitalism.

The rustic wooden sign hanging over the door of the bookstore was embellished with a painting of a beautiful nymph—long wavy hair and a gossamer gown. The garment was wrapped across one shoulder and streamed way below her feet, making it impossible for her to walk. But she had two butterfly wings near her shoulder blades so I guess she didn't need to. A wood nymph, a fairy? I had never believed in fairies, and whenever I saw pictures of them I felt left out—as if everyone knew about fairies but me.

The store was filled with old books, posters, wicker furniture, and stranger-looking spoons and utensils.

It smelled funny.

Marijuana, Eliot would have said.

Incense maybe, I would have replied.

"I want to show you something," Sidney said to Sally. He grabbed her hand and pulled her down a book-lined aisle.

Jesse headed for the gardening section. He selected a giant volume on growing organic vegetables, sat down cross-legged on the dirty floor, and was transported into a world of nitrogen, phosphorus, and potash.

Sidney and Sally must have found the erotica section. They were in a far corner, snickering and exclaiming. I poked through the history books. Maybe I'd get a book for Eliot. I came across one about John Winthrop, similar to the one I'd bought at Cannon Beach. "Oh, you bought a book for me," Eliot had said when he'd seen it. I had stared at him. He had walked away pleased that I had remembered him—which I hadn't, I don't think.

That had been a funny day too—wandering alone through the dusty bookstore in Cannon Beach. Alone and melancholy, but pleased with my melancholy. Today I felt alone too, but in a different way. Lonely and melancholy, yes, but also more depressed. Depressed and lonely.

THE evening performance was scheduled for 8:45. "We don't want to be late," Sidney said. "We might not find a place to sit. Besides, there's a Renaissance Fair before the play we don't want to miss."

I felt the irritation I always feel when someone is rushing me. Sidney was pacing in and out through the doorway of our motel room. "You look fine, Rebecca. Quit fussing."

I looked in the mirror. One eye was adorned with shadow and mascara, the other was lashless and pale. I turned to face Sidney.

"Oh, my gosh," he said. "Fix your other eye."

We arrived in plenty of time for the music fair. I watched the laughter and enjoyment of the Renaissance dancers with detached interest. *I should be enjoying this*, I thought.

After the show on the green we took our places within the half-timbered walls of the Elizabethan theater and I hoped it wouldn't get cold. I'd brought a light sweater, that was all.

It was almost time for the play to begin—*Macbeth*. I imagined the thin whine of a Scottish bagpipe and knew I would feel more at home watching *Macbeth* than I had watching the pleasure fair on the green.

The stage was dark. Thunder crashed and the play began as the three witches gabbled through their lines.

> *"Fair is foul, and foul is fair:*
> *Hover through the fog and filthy air."*

Jesse leaned over. "Have you seen this before?"

"No," I whispered back.

The action of the play continued and I got caught up in the drama. I watched as Macbeth paced back and forth across the stage pulling at the sides of his hair. His voice rang through the night air.

> *"Why do I yield to that suggestion*
> *Whose horrid image doth unfix my hair?"*

His ambition took cue from his imagination and he was drawn toward murder—his mind horrified by the things his imagination saw. The words were Macbeth's, but the voice was Eliot's—Eliot running his fingers through his hair. I couldn't believe it half the time myself. Why was I doing this?

"Overacting a bit, don't you think?" whispered Jesse. I ignored him and he turned to Sally. They whispered and giggled until I put my finger to my lips and said, "Shh." They looked at me as if seeing a strange apparition themselves, then continued to whisper and joke. On the stage Macbeth was changing his mind about murdering Duncan, and Lady Macbeth was wondering why she ever got involved.

> *"What beast was't then that made you break*
> *This enterprise to me?"*

Jesse leaned over again. "She's telling him she would do anything to help him further his career and now he wants to back out."

"Shut up," I said.

"She's just being the devoted, loving wife," Jesse continued.

"Jesse, would you just shut up? I'm trying to listen."

"Sor-ry," he said. He turned to Sally. I couldn't see his face, but Sally raised her eyebrows and shrugged her shoulders as if to say, "Don't ask me." She said something to Sidney, who leaned forward, eyeing me curiously. Sidney and Sally continued to whisper and giggle.

"Would you guys shut up?" I said, when my patience wore out. My voice was louder than I realized.

The woman behind me tapped me on the shoulder. She was leaning forward in the semidarkness and I could see she had her finger to her lips. "Shh," she said.

I pointed to Sidney and Sally. "It's them," I said. "They won't be quiet." I was no longer whispering.

"Rebecca," Jesse whispered, "lower your voice."

I glared at him. "I'm trying to listen and they won't be quiet," I said to the woman behind me.

She glanced at the man next to her and disappeared back into the darkness behind me, shaking her head and frowning.

"Idiot," I muttered.

Jesse looked at me in surprise, but I focused my eyes back on the stage and ignored him.

> *"I am in blood stepped in so far that, should I wade no more returning were as tedious as go o'er."*

There was no turning back. I can't undo what I did. Macbeth trudging toward his tragic end, Eliot pacing back and forth across our bedroom carpet.

"This is where Lady Macbeth starts coming unglued," Jesse whispered.

"Be quiet."

"She's a real basket case."

"Shut up."

Lady Macbeth was disintegrating before my eyes. Macbeth implored the doctor to do something.

> *Canst thou not minister to a mind diseased,*
> *Pluck from the memory a rooted sorrow,*
> *Raze out the written troubles of the brain,*
> *And with some sweet oblivious antidote*
> *Cleanse the stuffed bosom of that perilous stuff*
> *Which weighs upon the heart?*

Memory, a rooted sorrow, resentment—cleanse the stuffed bosom of that perilous stuff which weighs upon the heart.

> *"Therein the patient must minister to himself."*

A ROOTED SORROW

The words of the old doctor rang through the still night air and echoed against the half-timbered walls of the theater. I shivered and drew my sweater closer round my shoulders.

Therein the patient must minister to himself.

BIRNAM WOOD marched to Dunsinane. Macbeth was slain. The play ended, and as the Renaissance musicians played in the background, we filed from the theater.

We made the rounds of several beer gardens and pubs after that. Taverns, Eliot would have said.

Well, not taverns, exactly, I would have replied.

I tried some wine, but I didn't like it as well as the wine Lance and I had shared on the sand beside the pounding ocean. It was drier, not as sweet.

"Let's pick up a six-pack and go back to the motel," Sidney said.

I glanced at Jesse. He was along for the ride.

"I think I'd like some Seven-Up," I said.

"Oh, what do we have here? Rebecca of Sunnybrook Farm?" Sidney asked, clearly amused.

I glared at him.

We stopped at a Plaid Pantry and Sidney came out with two six-packs of beer, a half gallon of wine, and a ten-ounce can of Seven-Up.

Sally invited the guys to our room. They turned on the television and we started watching the late, late show. I was half-way through my can of Seven-Up when they finished the first six-pack.

"Here, Rebecca," Jesse said, "try a little wine in your Seven-Up. You might like that."

By the time they finished the second six-pack I was getting sleepy. Sidney poured each of us a glass of wine. I sipped at mine, but the others filled their glasses again and again. Jesse's eyes were red-rimmed and bleary. "I'm tired," he said at last. "I think I'm going to turn in. You coming, Sidney?"

"The movie's not over yet," Sidney said. "I want to see the end."

"Yeah, we want to see the end," chimed in Sally.

"Well, I'll shee you later. I'm goin' to bed."

He stumbled out the door.

After he left, I sat in the chair, my eyes focused on the television screen, trying to keep awake. Sidney and Sally were on Sally's bed. I tried not to notice what was going on over there. Finally I couldn't keep my eyes open any longer. "Come on, you guys," I said. "I want to go to bed. Why don't you two go to your room, Sidney? You have a TV." As if they were worried about the TV!

"Jesse's over there."

"Well, I'm here."

"Why don't you go to our room?" Sidney said.

"Forget it."

"Rebecca, believe me," Sidney said, waving his glass of wine in the air as he spoke, "with Jesse you don't have a thing to worry about." He put his arm around Sally and they giggled. "Besides," he said, his words slurring together and his head bobbing idiotically, "I dunno what you're so conshi-conshienshous about. Old Eliot wasn't so conshi-conshi—" He waved his hand through the air spastically. "—you know what I mean. He wasn't, was he?"

I stared at him. I could feel the blood drain from my face. My skin felt prickly and my knees buckled. I stumbled into the bathroom, locking the door behind myself. I leaned my back against the door.

So others did know. It wasn't my private shame after all.

I could hear the bedsprings squeaking. *Squeak, squeak.* Quiet . . . *squeak* . . . laughter . . . *squeak.* I couldn't stand it. Grasping the doorknob between my fingers, I yanked the bathroom door open. I rushed across the motel room and, without looking at the bed, jerked the outer door open and lunged outside. The cold nighttime air surrounded me, and the door locked itself behind me. I could hear Sidney and Sally giggling inside.

I shivered in the cold. I didn't have a plan—I just knew I couldn't stay in there any longer. I walked two doors down and knocked on Jesse's door.

"Jesse," I said, "open up. It's me, Rebecca." I waited, slapping my arms to keep warm, but nothing happened. "Jesse," I said, "open up."

"Hey, shut up out there," someone hollered from an adjoining room.

I grabbed the door knob and shook the door. "Open up, I'm freezing. Jesse, open up."

At last I heard movement inside. Jesse opened the door and stood blinking at me, leaning against the door for support.

"Do you have an extra blanket?" I said.

"Estra blanket? Wha' for?"

"Never mind, just give it to me." He stared at me, his eyes glazed. I wasn't sure he even recognized me. "Just go lie down," I said. "I'll get it myself." I found a blanket on the shelf in the closet. Jesse had plopped back onto the bed and was sound asleep, snoring, his mouth open. His long hair, no longer tied back, was spread across the pillow in dark waves and I could barely see the earring glinting on his earlobe. I turned out the light but hesitated in the doorway. Better make sure the car wasn't locked. I put the blanket in the doorway to keep the door from locking and checked the doors of Sidney's car. Unlocked. I sighed in relief.

I pulled the blanket from the door and listened to the lock click into place behind me.

I curled up in the backseat of Sidney's Volkswagen and pulled the blanket tight around me. I slept a little, off and on, but it was cold and cramped.

Several drunks hollered and pounded on the door of a room across the way. I sat up to see what was going on. One of them saw me.

"Hey, what's going on here?" he said, starting across the parking lot and waving for the others to follow. I rechecked the locks on the doors and scrunched as low as I could in the backseat, pulling the blanket around my neck. I could hear their voices getting louder, shouting obscenities, as they came closer to the car. Suddenly, pressed against the glass of the window opposite me, was a face as grotesque as a gargoyle. I jammed my knuckles into my teeth to keep from screaming.

"What are you doing in there, sweetie?"

"Want some company?"

Soon there were four or five faces peering at me through the windows of the Volkswagen as they began rocking the car. They stood on the bumpers, jumping up and down, laughing and joking. I imagined them tipping the car over or breaking one of the windows. I could feel their strong arms pulling me from the car, their fingers pressed into my flesh and their gargoyle lips pressed against my face. What if they got to me somehow, touching me, hurting me, leaving me raped and bruised in the backseat of the Volkswagen?

Finally someone called to them from across the way and they wandered back across the parking lot, singing and shouting.

"Bye, sweetheart."

"Sorry we couldn't get better acquainted."

I heard their voices a little longer and then they faded and I heard the slam of a door. They must have gone inside one of the rooms. I clamped my arms against my breast and lay in the back of the car shaking and wanting to cry, but unable to. Should I get out and try to get back into our room? What if I couldn't get in? Jesse was no help. Hadn't Sidney and Sally heard the commotion? Didn't they wonder where I was?

I was afraid of being stranded between the car and the motel room—being caught by the men from across the way—so I scrunched myself together in the dark cold quiet of Sidney's Volkswagen and tried to sleep. But all night long cars drove in and out of the parking lot and I could hear men's voices shouting and laughing. Brakes squealed and tires screeched along the nearby street.

I thought of the gargoyle faces pressed against the window and remembered Eliot's words. *I don't like it, Rebecca. I just don't like it.* Men's voices loud and confident. *What are you doing in there sweetie? I forbid it, you can't go.* Strong arms pulling me from the car, gargoyle lips pressing against my face. What did he mean, forbid it? He couldn't forbid it.

What was all this nonsense about equality? There was no equality. They were bigger and stronger and meaner. They could beat us and rape us and force us by their sheer strength. It was a farce, a concession. *That's right, girls, you're equal, sure you are, don't let anyone tell you differently.*

It needed to be measured. We needed to gauge and carefully chart their physical might against our strengths in other areas—intellect, intuition, sensitivity. We needed to prove there were areas in which we were superior, balance our strong points and our weak points, keep things even, equal.

. . . did not consider equality something to be grasped . . . made himself nothing.

I squeezed my eyes together. What did it matter? What did any of it matter? What did it matter if men were superior, or if they just thought they were? What did it matter if we were all equal or if we were living in the remnants of a mind-boggling hierarchy? If we were all called to submission by God—called by God to submit to him and to one another—then what did any of it matter?

I pulled the blanket tightly around my shoulders. Jesus hadn't seemed worried about equality—not about his own anyway. *In very nature God . . . did not grasp at equality . . . took on the nature of a servant.*

We were all called to become like Christ—to be conformed to his image—to become servants. That had to be it. That was the secret. Servanthood. That had to be the answer. Servanthood was the only answer.

ABOUT an hour after sunrise I crawled, aching and stiff from the Volkswagen, and walked to the nearby restaurant for a cup of coffee. By the time I got back to the motel, Sidney was loading things into the car. Sally limped out the motel door.

"I've gotten most of my things, Rebecca. I think the rest are yours."

"OK," I said.

Jesse stumbled from his room with his duffle bag and tossed it into the trunk in silence. Nobody bothered to ask where I'd spent the night. They just stumbled about bleary-eyed and silent until we were packed and ready to leave.

"We'll drive for an hour or so, then stop for breakfast and coffee," Sidney said.

"Hmm."

We piled into the car and Sidney followed the signs directing us to Interstate 5, North.

We were silent. All of us. Then I sneezed. Nobody said gesundheit. Even Eliot would have said gesundheit. I sneezed again, then again.

"Does anyone have a Kleenex?" I said.

Nobody even bothered to look. "No," they muttered.

Nobody had a Kleenex. That figured. Nobody even had a Kleenex.

CHAPTER 25

BY the time I got home from Ashland, I felt like Lady Macbeth—I was disintegrating. I offered no information about my weekend, and Eliot didn't ask any questions. When I awoke Sunday morning it was raining, and water was gushing over the edge of the downspout. Eliot hadn't cleaned the gutters in the fall, and the sound of the rushing water made me uneasy. When I got up and looked out the window I could see it pouring over the top of the gutters and cascading to the ground. It flowed across the grass in rivulets that would leave bald spots in the lawn.

Bed, had to get back to bed, felt funny. I crawled back in bed and pulled the pillow over my head.

"REBECCA, Rebecca." It was Eliot, calling my name, almost a whisper. I opened my eyes briefly. Light. The pain was excruciating. I clamped my eyelids shut and winced. My head expanded and contracted in waves of pain. My muscles ached, even my bones ached. "Can you eat a piece of toast?" I shook my head, then was sorry I'd moved. Pain rolled from one side of my head to the other.

I SLEPT most of the day. *Rebecca, Rebecca.* Sometimes I heard Eliot calling my name and opened my eyes, expecting to see him beside my bed, only to realize I'd been dreaming. Other times I thought I was dreaming and would realize Eliot was brushing his fingers through my hair, softly whispering my name. *Rebecca, Rebecca.*

Since I slept most of the day, I didn't expect to sleep that night, but I did. I wasn't as aware of the pain.

Monday morning I woke late. Eliot was beside the bed with tea and toast.

"You'd better eat something," he said.

"I'm not hungry."

"Here, just have a bite of toast." He sat on the edge of the bed and held the toast to my mouth. I took a tiny bite and felt my stomach churn. I shook my head and pushed his hand away.

"Some tea?"

I shook my head again. I wanted him to leave me alone, but be there. Not talk to me or shove food at me, just be there. He stayed there most of the morning, brushing his fingers through my hair, not talking. I slipped in and out of sleep. . . .

The witches chanted and Macbeth paced back and forth pulling at the side of his hair. Fair is foul and foul is fair, hover through the fog and filthy air. Canst thou not minister to a mind diseased? Pluck from the memory a rooted sorrow? *Against a wavy background I saw Eliot leading a man toward my bed, a man dressed in white with a stethoscope around his neck. The man shook his head sadly. Eliot asked him if he was sure and the doctor nodded.* Therein the patient must minister to himself. Whose horrid image doth unfix my hair. . . . *Unfix my hair. I screamed and grabbed at the fingers running through my hair. I pierced the unwanted hands with my sharp fingernails.*

"Rebecca, Rebecca, it's all right, it's all right."

I opened my eyes and let go of Eliot's hands. One of them was bleeding where I had scratched him. "Was the doctor here?"

"No, no. I called him and he said it's just the flu. There's a lot of it going around, but I don't understand why it's hit you so hard. I've never seen you so sick. When did you start feeling badly? Were you sick in Ashland?"

I shook my head. "On the way home . . . started Friday night . . . couldn't get warm."

"Where were you? Some flea-trap motel with no heat?"

"Sidney's Volkswagen."

"Sidney's Volkswagen! What the—?"

I held up my hand. Eliot was pacing back and forth across the bedroom by then. I tried to sit up, thinking I could explain things better sitting up, but the pain forced my head back onto the pillow. I closed my eyes. "Stop pacing," I said. "Makes my head hurt." Eliot stopped beside the bed. I brushed the hair from my forehead and said, "Jesse was drunk and went to bed and I was too tired to stay awake any longer . . . Sidney and Sally wouldn't get off the bed, and I went in the bathroom—"

I started to cry. Eliot handed me a Kleenex. "Sidney said why didn't I just go over with Jesse . . . Eliot wasn't so conscientious." I burst into a fresh round of sobs, and Eliot took me in his arms. I wiped my nose on his shirt sleeve. "So I knew he knew about you and Sylvia. I ran out of the room and was locked out and couldn't get Jesse to wake up . . . someone was yelling at me and Jesse finally woke up and I got a blanket from him. He was drunk, and then I crawled in the backseat of Sidney's Volkswagen. It was so cold . . . and these drunks came . . . and I thought they were going to tip the car over. They were shouting and jumping on the car and Sidney didn't even come out to see what was the matter . . . or if I was all right . . . nobody even cared where I was. . . ."

I wasn't making much sense, but Eliot got the picture. He started pacing about the room again. "If that creep had one shred of common sense . . ." He slammed the box of Kleenex on the floor. "All night in his car? No wonder you got sick." I closed my eyes and turned away from him, easing my head deeper into the pillow. "I'd like to—I feel like wringing the guy's neck," he said.

I put my arm across my eyes. "Eliot, please," I said, "the pacing—my head."

He stopped beside the bed again. My head was turned from him and I kept my eyes closed. He stood there, motionless and quiet, for some time. Then I felt him adjusting the blankets closer around my neck. He brushed a few straggles of hair from my forehead and kissed me on the cheek. "Try to get some sleep," he said.

When I awoke, the house was quiet and it was still raining. Eliot was beside the bed, and I could hear the water pouring over the downspout and onto the ground. I opened my eyes. "Where are the children?"

"At school."

"School? What day is it? Monday? Why aren't you at school?"

"I stayed home."

Eliot stayed home? Eliot never stayed home, ever.

"Can I get you anything?"

"Ice, crushed ice."

Eliot crushed some ice and brought it to me in a juice glass. I chewed on the ice a teaspoonful at a time.

I slept most of the afternoon.

The next morning I felt better, but Eliot insisted on staying home with me.

"You'd better get back to your classes."

"They'll be fine."

I was able to eat a little and Eliot hovered beside the bed. "What sounds good? Toast, applesauce?"

"Applesauce."

He brought me a small dish of applesauce and stayed nearby till I finished it.

WEDNESDAY morning I felt well enough to go downstairs. Eliot and the children were finishing their breakfast when I walked into the kitchen, and I was afraid someone would speak to me. Nobody did. I fixed myself a bowl of Grape-nuts and sat at the table crunching them. I knew I was driving Eliot crazy with my munching. I reached across the table for the newspaper and carelessly knocked over the carton of milk. The milk spread across the tabletop. Shelly righted the milk carton, and I continued to crunch my cereal as I skimmed the front page of the paper. The pool of milk expanded until it reached the crack in the center of the table when it began a steady drip to the floor. I felt the splash, splash, splash of milk on my fuzzy slippers.

I continued to crunch my cereal.

Without a word, Eliot grabbed a couple of towels and began mopping up the milk. I could feel the soft terry cloth against my foot as he wiped the milk from my slipper. I continued munching my cereal as he knelt on the floor beneath our table, wiping the milk from my feet.

I finished my Grape-nuts and went back upstairs. I probed my way back to bed, sinking gratefully onto the mattress. I heard Eliot leave for school and then the children. I was alone and the house was quiet and it was still raining. The rain washed over the house and over the trees, cleansing the landscape, the grass and soil. I pressed my head into the pillow and my tears washed over my face. I cried and cried and had no idea why. *What God? What?*

Forgive and you shall be forgiven.

What? Forgiveness? Such an outlandish thing.

I reached to my nightstand. Where was my Bible? Hadn't seen it in months, hadn't bothered to read it. I opened the top drawer and it wasn't there. The second drawer—not there either. I patted the floor under the bed with my hand. Nope.

I rolled to Eliot's side of the bed and opened the drawer of his nightstand. I could use Eliot's Bible. Eliot's Bible with its pristine pages. It was unmarked, no notes. We had always disagreed about writing in Bibles. I had always written all over mine, underlining verses and making little notes to myself if something seemed important. But Eliot had always refused to make a mark in his. "I want it fresh from God each time," he said, "not cluttered with my own ideas." A purist.

I lifted it from the drawer and flipped through the pages, clean and white and unmarked.

But suddenly something caught my eye—a flash of red. As I had flipped through the pages there had been a flicker of scarlet. I leafed through the pages again but couldn't find it. Something underlined in red? In Eliot's Bible? I held my finger to the pages and let them sift by slowly, one by one. It was there—something—I knew I'd seen something. The pages whispered against each other, one after the other, but I couldn't find it. Oh, well, what did it matter? Wait, there it was, back a few pages. There—a psalm, Psalm 32, underlined in red. And there was a short notation, in Eliot's writing, and a date. I squinted my eyes—*January 20th*. A pain gnawed at my stomach. Eliot's birthday.

> *Dear Father,*
> *I accept your forgiveness.*
> *Thank you.*

Then a little farther down, so tiny I could barely make it out, was my name, followed by a question mark.

> *What about Rebecca—will she ever forgive me?*

Well, what about me? What did it matter about me? Eliot had just gone ahead and gotten himself forgiven by God. How could God do that? But he still wanted mine. I still had the power to withhold my forgiveness—torturing Eliot and myself with my resentment—hanging onto it and milking it for all it was worth . . . which wasn't much. It wasn't worth much. Suddenly it seemed like a puny, ugly scrap of a thing—my unforgiveness. In the presence of God's unbounded grace and love and acceptance I felt as if I held inside my bosom a creeping, slimy creature nobody in his right mind would cling to.

I smashed my face into my pillow and sobbed. I could hear my own sobs in the quiet of the deserted house and they sounded strange to me—as if they belonged to someone else. I cried to God aloud and sobbed and when I heard myself I wondered if I were going mad. I saw myself, wet with tears, tossing and turning in the twisted sheets of Eliot's and my bed. *Forgive and ye shall be forgiven*. I saw the me of long ago, the cherished me, crumbling beneath the boots of Eliot's betrayal. I saw my wall, my memorial wall, crumbling beneath the hand of love, and I cried out in fear and dread and hope.

And then I slept.

When I awoke it had stopped raining and I was hungry. I went downstairs, and just as I entered the kitchen the phone rang. It was Alison.

"How are you? Eliot said you were really sick."

"I'm better. I was just getting myself something to eat."

"Well, I won't keep you, you probably want to get back to bed. I just wanted you to know I was thinking about you . . . praying for you."

Praying for me? I was glad to know someone was praying for me. "Thanks."

I stayed home Thursday too. I thought Sidney or Jesse might call to check on me, but they didn't. Marlene came by with dinner—our whole dinner. She'd heard I was sick so she brought over a casserole, a salad, and a loaf of bread. And a pie. I couldn't believe it—a homemade pie.

I wanted to sneer at her homemade bread and her pie with its flaky crust, but I couldn't, because it all looked so good and I was so hungry, and I was sure Shelly would have fixed TV dinners that night. I wanted to sneer again when she said they'd remember to pray for me at Bible study. "Forget it," I wanted to shout. "Forget it. I don't want to be served up as a prayer request at your silly Bible study." But I couldn't say that either. Because I wanted them to pray for me. I did. I wanted them to pray for me.

As she was leaving, Marlene lingered awkwardly at the door. "Rebecca," she said, "I've been thinking about what I said Easter morning—about you being a feminist." I stared at her, speechless. Did we have to discuss this now? My knees still felt weak, and I propped myself up against the door frame. Marlene continued. "I don't think I should have said what I did. I get a little carried away sometimes."

I was slumped against the doorway and I nodded my head. "That's OK. It's . . . confusing."

FRIDAY morning I felt much better. I toyed with the idea of going back to school. Alison called early, while I was still in bed.

"How are you feeling?"

"Pretty good."

"Are you going to school?"

"I don't know. I'm not sure I could make it all day."

"Hmm."

"Why?"

"Oh, well, I just thought if you were feeling up to it you might like to come to Bible study this morning."

Bible study? Go to a women's Bible study?

I started to say no, then, for some reason, changed my mind and agreed to go. But after I hung up the phone I considered calling her back to tell her I didn't feel well after all.

But I wanted to go. Part of me did.

IT had been almost a year since I had last attended Bible study. In that time many of the faces had already changed. But Marlene was there, of course, and Martha, and two or three others I recognized.

A brunette and a gray-haired woman standing nearby were talking about a mutual friend who wasn't a believer. "I've been praying for her," the brunette said. "She doesn't seem to have a chance." The gray-haired woman agreed. When she turned and saw me she was strangely quiet. A newcomer. *Here's another one,* she was thinking—*an unbeliever.*

Vultures. That's what they reminded me of. I doubted that God looked down on me like that. Even though I might see myself as a naughty sheep, going my own way, scampering across the fields and falling into crevices, I never imagined God coming down on me with talons extended, gloating over my predicament. I still saw him as a shepherd—the good shepherd gently prodding his willful sheep toward the fold.

As the Bible study began I realized that although some of the faces had changed, they were still discussing the same topic.

"Don't forget that although God looks on the heart, man still looks on the outward appearance," Martha was saying. "It's important to keep ourselves attractive. It makes it easier for our husbands to love us."

One girl, short, blonde, and obviously pregnant said, "But what I don't understand is, if Christ loves us no matter what, and our husbands are supposed to love us like Christ loves the Church, then why . . ."

Martha smiled at her. It was the same smile she had smiled at me in what now seemed like a lifetime ago—patient and condescending. She raised her eyebrow slightly as she spoke. "But do they? Is it really possible for them to love us the way Christ loves the Church?"

I felt warm from head to toe. My eyes filled with tears, and I could feel my forehead damp with perspiration. Martha's living room was closing in around me, and for a moment everything in the room was drained of color. Everything was black and white, but backwards, like a photograph negative. Peoples' faces were black while their hair and eye sockets, even the shadows in their ears, were white and glaring. There was a buzzing in my ears and I blinked my eyes to bring things back into focus.

But then bursting across my vision came a picture in vivid color. It was a field and there were mountains and trees and green grass. There was a bubbling brook. There were sheep, millions and millions of sheep. Some were standing quietly munching grass, others were heading for the gurgling creek. Still others were running willfully toward a steep crevice. But wandering around among the sheep, unhurried, was a gentle shepherd. He would call to his sheep and some would come quickly to his side. Others would scamper away. He would follow after the erring sheep, calling their names. Calling them by name. If they didn't listen, he would prod them gently with his staff, prod them back into the safety of the fold. But always calling them by name. The gentle prodding shepherd. My sheep hear my voice. *Rebecca, Rebecca.*

The green fields disappeared. The vision of the sheep and the shepherd disappeared. And then, for a brief moment I saw Eliot. He was wiping milk from my fuzzy slipper. He was washing my feet, washing my feet like Christ washing the feet of his disciples—not accusing, not screaming at me that I needed to be more careful, just patiently cleaning up the mess I'd made.

"Sometimes," I whispered.

Martha turned toward me. "What? What was that Rebecca?"

"Sometimes," I repeated.

"Sometimes what, dear?"

I looked up. I stared at Martha and then at the faces of the other women staring back at me. I cleared my throat and stared down at my hands. My fingers were squeezed together and my left thumb was pressed on my right knuckle. I could feel my skin drawn tightly over the tendons. Beneath the sinews I could feel the hardness of bone. I looked fiercely into Martha's face. "Sometimes they do love us that way," I said. "Sometimes they do love us the way Christ loves the Church."

Martha cleared her throat. "Well, yes, I suppose so, but it's not something we can count on. We can't count on them to love us like that."

"But sometimes they do," I repeated.

Martha was silent a moment. She looked into my eyes. I stared back into hers. It seemed that we saw each other for the first time. Her eyes softened. "I guess what I was trying to say, Rebecca, was that sometimes they love us with Christlike love and sometimes they don't. The times they do are not the problem. It's the times they don't that we have trouble with. It's when they don't love us the way they should that we are left with the difficult choice." Her voice was soft.

I gazed into her eyes. "What choice is that?" I asked.

She looked deep into my eyes. "The choice," she said, "whether or not to forgive them."

My eyes involuntarily traveled to Alison. She was watching me with steadfast calm.

I lowered my head.

Oh, *that* choice.

CHAPTER 26

WHEN Alison dropped me off at my home after Bible study, I still felt a little feverish. I went upstairs to our bedroom. Perhaps I would take a nap. I sat on the edge of the bed, on Eliot's side, and held my face in my hands. "O God," I said. "What?"

I sat there quietly. The silence in the room pressed against me. It prodded and shoved at me, nudging me. What? What?

I reached in Eliot's drawer for his Bible. I turned the whispering pages to Psalm 32, underlined in red.

> *When I kept silent about my sin,*
> *my body wasted away*
> *Through my groaning all day long.*
> *For day and night Thy hand was heavy upon me;*
> *My vitality was drained away*
> *as with the fever-heat of summer.*
> *I acknowledged my sin to Thee,*
> *And my iniquity I did not hide.*
> *I said, "I will confess my transgressions to the Lord,"*
> *And Thou didst forgive the guilt of my sin.*

I stared at the words until they blurred into a misty gray. Tears fell onto the pages and I tried to brush them away without smearing the red ink. I fell to my knees beside the bed, Eliot's Bible open before me. I pressed my forehead against the quilted bedspread. "Oh, Father God, please forgive me. Please forgive me for my hard, unforgiving heart."

As my fingers touched the pages of Eliot's Bible, I saw myself pretending to be the perfect wife. And then I remembered our empty shell of a marriage. "Forgive me for trying to trick Eliot into loving me. I'm sorry for building a wall around myself when my tricks didn't work. I was so angry! Teach me how to be honest and loving. Help me to stand firm in my identity as your child. I have dignity and worth in you. I don't want to have to connive ways to win his—or anyone's—approval. I want to be so secure in your love that I won't have to grasp at things—at being equal. Help me, God!"

My mind went quiet for awhile and then a new rush of words poured out. "Father, I have been selfish. I don't think that I once thought about what sort of pain drove Eliot to do what he did, or what kind of guilt he felt afterward—only myself, only my pain. I've given no thought to the children's needs for so long—only my needs. I haven't even thought of you, God. I guess I couldn't stand your presence. Oh, I am so sorry.

"I guess we all need to be forgiven. Lord, I'm just tired of trying to excuse myself. I'm tired of trying to decide who is right, and who is wrong. I've worn myself out trying to believe that it was all Eliot's doing. It doesn't matter. We can't sort it all out. All we can do is throw ourselves at your feet—and at each other's feet."

I shifted my knees. My legs were falling asleep. "O God, I understand now that Eliot couldn't go back and undo what he did. I can't go back and see what I didn't see. I didn't see my own callousness and selfishness. I didn't see any of it. All I saw was that Eliot had hurt me and that I wasn't going to let him hurt me again. That's what I saw and that's what I acted on. I can't change any of it. But Father God, I confess it to you and throw myself at your feet, because there's nothing else I can do.

"This is a crooked, bent world, and we have crooked, bent personalities. All we can do is ask for forgiveness, from you and from each other. Because we'll never do it right. We'll never do it all right."

I paused. The words had been bubbling from my lips in a soft mur-

mur. Now they stopped. I felt a tightening in my throat. I gripped my fingers into the bedspread. I squeezed them together until I could feel the tips of my fingernails bending and curling into the spread. The tightness in my throat spread down and into my chest.

"Father God," I whispered. My words stopped again, faded into silence. I waited quietly. The tightness in my chest grew. I doubled over, folding my arms around myself, until I was sitting on the floor in a tight knot. I reached for Eliot's Bible. My head was bent forward and my arms were pressed tight against my stomach, squeezing the Bible.

"Dear Father God," I said in a whisper, "Dear Father God, I forgive . . . I forgive Eliot." I was silent. "I forgive him, God."

A sob broke loose from the center of the tightness and ripped its way to freedom. Fresh tears poured down my face and onto the pages of Eliot's Bible. I brushed them aside with my hand. I sobbed until the tenseness in my body was washed away.

Some of my tears had mingled with the red ink on the page of Eliot's Bible, and the movement of my hand made an ugly slash of red on the pristine surface.

After my tears had stopped, I folded my hands lightly in my lap and sat beside the bed in silence. I closed my eyes and leaned my body against the bed. The stillness of the room was all around me, and the quietness of my soul was within. And I sat in the hushed presence of my God until I heard the front door open and Matthew's eleven-year-old voice ringing through my sanctuary.

"We're home. Is there anything to eat?"

CHAPTER 27

I WAS anxious to talk to Eliot—I hadn't really talked to him for a year and a half. But that evening was Tyler's spring concert—twenty-eight first-graders singing twenty-eight little songs:

Ten little speckled frogs
Sat on a speckled log
Eating some most delicious bugs—
Yum, yum, yum.

As soon as we got home, Eliot plopped in front of the TV and became engrossed in a movie.

The time didn't seem right.

The next morning Mother telephoned and invited us to the farm. Going to the farm was getting easier. I no longer felt a knot of pain in the pit of my stomach when I saw the roof of Daddy's barn poke itself onto the horizon.

Mother was flighty as she served the children their customary cookies and milk. Then she sent them outside to play, leaving Eliot, Mother, and me at the kitchen table alone. We chatted for awhile, but the conversation didn't get anywhere. Mother kept asking us questions, and when we answered she said, "Hmm, uh-huh," while her mind drifted elsewhere. Finally she glanced at Eliot uneasily. "Would you like some coffee, Eliot?"

Eliot shifted in his chair. An invitation to stay or a suggestion he leave? Eliot decided to leave.

"I think I'll go play ball with the boys," he said.

As soon as he was gone, Mother rose to turn on the burner beneath her teakettle. "I've found a buyer for the farm," she said, her back to me.

A buyer for the farm?

I rose and moved to the sink, where I stood staring out the window of Mother's spotless kitchen. The house smelled like Ivory soap again. All of it. Even the bedroom.

"Rebecca, I know how much this farm means to you. I would never want to sell it if I felt you or Susan . . ."

I gazed out the window toward the orchard and my tree. "Have you talked to Susan?"

She shook her head.

"We both love the farm . . . and we'll miss it. But we don't expect you to stay here and babysit our past for us."

Mother reached for the box of Kleenex she always kept on the counter and pulled one out. "It's just so hard. . . ." She paused to blow her nose. "It's just so hard to change."

I put my arm around her and pulled her close. "I know," I whispered. "I know."

WHILE Mother fussed with dinner I went outside to find Eliot. I wanted to show him something. He was having a game of cowboys and Indians with Matthew and Tyler. I waved to him and he walked toward me. Matthew ran up behind him. "Mom," he said, "I've been wanting to ask you something."

"What?"

"Why do doctors and nurses wear masks?"

Doctors and nurses. Was he still thinking about when Daddy was in the hospital? It was so hard to know what was going on in their minds.

"Well, Matthew," I began. "You know about germs, don't you, how they—"

Matthew laughed. "No, no, Mom. It's so if someone makes a mistake no one will know who did it."

He ran away, pointing a finger at me and my stupidity. I turned to Eliot. "I will never learn," I said.

"Don't feel bad," he said. "I fell for it too."

I took Eliot's hand. "Come with me," I said. "I want to show you something."

I had never told Eliot about my tree, ever. In the eighteen years of our marriage I had never mentioned that I had a special tree—a place to dream when my mind was whisked into the clouds, and a place to cry when disappointment thumped me back to earth.

It was time to show it to him.

I led Eliot through the orchard and to my tree. "I came here after Daddy died," I said. "It's where I always used to come to cry." I leaned against my tree and rubbed my hand back and forth across the scratchy bark. I moved back from my tree and let my eyes wander up the trunk and into the branches. "It will seem strange without it," I said.

"Without it?"

I leaned against the tree again. "Mother's selling the farm," I said.

"O-oh," Eliot said, nodding his head. "So that's what was on her mind." He studied my face. "Are you upset? Is that going to bother you?"

I shook my head. "It's OK. It's only logical—it's just that everything seems to be changing at once. Nothing's the same anymore—Daddy's gone, the farm, my tree and . . . and . . ." I lowered my head and I could feel tears forming behind my eyes.

"And what?"

I shook my head.

"And us?" Eliot said.

I stared at the ground. The orchard had been plowed recently—Mr. Bellows was right on schedule—but there was tall spring grass growing close to the trunk of my tree. I pressed the grass against the ground and sat on the springy softness, my back against the tree trunk. Eliot sat beside me.

"I guess so," I said.

"Change isn't always bad, Rebecca."

"But sometimes it is."

"It doesn't have to be."

"But how do you make it good? How do you make things start getting better instead of worse?"

"By starting where you are—admitting where you are."

I picked a long stem of grass and pressed it between my lips, sucking the sweetness. I leaned my head against the bark of my apple tree and stared at the earth and the grass, and at the sky through the leaves. "Where are we?" I said.

"I'll tell you where I am," Eliot said, after a moment's quiet. "I'm sitting beneath an apple tree with the woman I love. I've known and loved her for twenty years, but she has never before shown me her special place—the place she runs to when things hurt too badly. I've learned something new about her and I love the new thing I've learned—because it's real. We've had a lot of things muddying up our relationship, Rebecca—a lot of stupid roles and pretensions and . . . and just junk, but I love you. When I see the real you, I love you with a love I can't even describe."

Tears were stinging my eyes and I blinked, staring at the branches patterned against the sky without looking at Eliot. "I was snooping through your Bible the other day," I said.

Eliot became very still. "And?"

"I thought you didn't believe in marking your Bible."

"I didn't."

"What changed your mind?"

"Something important."

"What?"

"Rebecca," he said, "do you have any idea what it's like to see your own guilt—see it—and know there isn't anything you can do to make it go away?" He cleared his throat. His eyes burned into mine with a light I couldn't label—pain or joy. "Do you know what it's like to realize there is absolutely nothing you can do? That all you can do is ask for mercy?—for forgiveness?" His eyes searched mine. "Do you have any idea what that's like?"

I lowered my head and nodded, tears spilling down my cheeks.

"Yes," I whispered. I was silent a moment. "Eliot," I said, wiping my nose with the back of my hand and looking into his eyes, "I just . . . I just couldn't forgive you. I felt so alone, so betrayed. I . . . I just couldn't."

He pressed my head against his shoulder. "Oh, Rebecca, Rebecca, I'm so sorry. I'm so sorry."

"But I have now," I whispered. "I have." I lifted my head and looked into his face. "I've forgiven you."

I moved my body against his. His embrace obliterated everything except the awareness of his body against mine and the comfort of our union. He pressed my face against his cheek and I felt my tears intermingling with his. "Thank you," he whispered, "thank you . . . thank you."

CHAPTER
28

MONDAY morning I returned to classes. I was still angry with Sidney and Jesse and I dreaded drama class. When I arrived, Jesse wasn't there yet. That was good. I didn't have to decide whether to sit next to him or not. Let him decide. I seated myself and opened my psychology text. I was terribly behind in my reading. Besides, if I looked busy I would have an excuse for not speaking to him. Sidney wasn't there yet either, but Sidney was almost always late, and because he was teaching I didn't face the same awkwardness I did with Jesse. I buried my head in the psych book.

When Jesse arrived he plopped into the desk next to mine as if nothing were the matter.

"Hi, Rebecca."

I glanced up. "Hi."

"Where have you been?"

"I was sick." Clipped tone. Eyes back to my book.

"Did you have the flu? A whole week. That's a long t-time to be sick."

"I guess it was the flu. It started out with a cold. It felt like pneumonia. I thought I was going to die." Eyes back to my book.

"Come on, it w-wasn't that bad."

"It was awful."

He looked at me, puzzled. "What's the matter? You act like you're mad about being sick. Everyone gets s-sick once in awhile." He shrugged his shoulders expansively. "We won't hold it against you."

I pressed my lips together and didn't look at him.

"Rebecca, what's the deal? Why are you upset? Did I do something? Are you m-mad at me?"

I stared ahead for a moment and then turned to face Jesse. My lips were close together as I spoke. "The reason I got sick, Jesse, was that I spent Friday night in Sidney's Volkswagen and I nearly froze to death. That's why I got sick. And yes I am m-mad at you." I stared straight ahead again.

I shouldn't have done that. I shouldn't have imitated his stutter.

"You spent the night in the c-car? How come?"

"Because I couldn't get Sidney to leave our room and I was exhausted, that's why."

"Well, why didn't you say something? I'd have made him leave."

I pressed my hand to my breast and leaned forward. "You? You would have made him leave? Jesse, you were passed out on your bed." I looked at him quizzically. "You don't even remember me coming in for a blanket, do you?"

"A blanket?"

"Brother!" I said, and turned away.

Sidney entered the room, and after clearing his throat several times, began the session. I focused my eyes just over the top of his head for the entire hour. As soon as class was over I rose from my desk and headed for the door.

"Rebecca, wait," Jesse called. "Sidney, come here." Jesse stood by his desk like a traffic cop, waving one arm for me to come back and the other for Sidney to come over. I stopped and turned around, but I didn't move toward him. Jesse grabbed Sidney by the elbow and pulled him toward me. "Rebecca's m-mad at us, Sidney," he said.

"Where've you been, Rebecca?" Sidney said. "We thought you'd dropped off the earth."

"I was on my deathbed," I said. There was a pout in my voice, a perfect little pout, and I wasn't even trying.

"You must have really been sick. You missed a whole week of school."

Jesse was standing in silence. He was watching me closely, waiting for me to light into Sidney. I decided not to disappoint him. "I got sick," I said, and I could feel tiny lightning bolts of anger flashing from my eyes, "because I spent last Friday night in your Volkswagen. I nearly froze to death."

Sidney stared at me in disbelief. "You what? You spent the night in the car?"

"Well, where did you think I spent the night?" I said. "I couldn't sleep in our room with you and Sally carrying on."

Sidney scratched his head and glanced at Jesse. "Well, I guess I thought you—" he nodded his head toward Jesse, "—I thought you went over to our room."

"Oh, brother," I said. I folded my arms across my chest.

Jesse shifted from one foot to the other, folded his arms, and then unfolded them, letting them hang awkwardly at the sides of his body.

"You guys didn't even care," I said. "Neither of you even gave a thought to where I was or what was happening to me. I could have been kidnapped or murdered or something. I can't believe that. You didn't even wonder where I was."

Sidney held out his hand. "Look, Rebecca, we had a little too much to drink, that's all."

"You can say that again."

"We just got a little carried away. Can you forgive us?"

"Yeah, w-will you forgive us, Rebecca?" Jesse chimed in.

They both stood there sheepishly, their heads hanging slightly, waiting for my reply. Forgive? Forgive them? Was this for real?

"I could have died of pneumonia," I said.

"We know, Rebecca. It was awful; it was an awful thing we did."

"Yeah, it was. It was awful. W-will you forgive us?"

I stared at the two of them as they stood there waiting—Sidney with his lonesome, shifty eyes and Jesse with his absurd ponytail and glittering earring. They were half-serious, half-joking, but the fact remained, they were standing there waiting—waiting for me to forgive them.

Forgive and you shall be forgiven.

For some reason it seemed more outlandish to forgive Sidney and Jesse for allowing me to sleep in the VW all night than it did to forgive

Eliot for his adultery. Not harder—just more outlandish.

I moved the toe of my shoe back and forth on the tile floor, staring at it thoughtfully. Finally I lifted my head. "Oh, all right," I said. "I forgive you—you big dummies."

"Hurray," Jesse shouted. He slapped Sidney across the shoulders. "Let's go get a cup of coffee to celebrate our forgiveness. I don't know if I've ever been forgiven before."

I hesitated.

"Come on," Sidney said, grabbing me by the elbow. "Come on. Jesse and I will even buy, won't we, Jesse?"

"We will?" Jesse said. He stuck his hand in his jeans pocket and pulled out his change, counting it quickly. "Yeah," he said. "We will. We'll buy."

"You're kidding," I said. "Well, all right! All right!"

WE had only been in the coffee shop a few minutes when I looked up to see Eliot enter. He stopped in the doorway and stared at us. Then he headed toward our table. His boots made a thudding sound as he walked across the coffee shop. He stood beside our table, towering over us, glaring. We all looked up at him expectantly, as we might have looked at the sky, waiting for a thunderclap. Nobody said a word. I couldn't stand it.

I cleared my throat. "I told Eliot about spending the night in the car," I said, glancing at Sidney. "He wasn't very happy."

Sidney rose to his feet. "I don't blame you, Eliot. It was irresponsible." He held out his hand. His face was serious. "I've already apologized to Rebecca. I want to apologize to you too." He stood there with his hand out. Eliot stared back at him.

I could almost read Eliot's mind. *Romping with your students while my wife is catching pneumonia.* He continued to stare at Sidney.

Take his hand. Take his hand. Sidney's face began to harden, but still he held out his hand. He looked straight into Eliot's eyes, and he smiled slightly, an almost fiendish smile, as only Sidney could do.

"Well," Sidney said, still standing there with his hand out, "none of us is perfect, isn't that right, Eliot?"

The muscles along Eliot's cheekbones contracted slightly. He stared hard into the eyes of Sidney Wolfe.

We can only be forgiven. All of us. None of us can do it right. Not all the time.

Eliot's face relaxed. "You're right, Wolfe," he said, extending his hand. "You're right."

They shook hands. Then Eliot turned and extended his hand to Jesse—Jesse with his ponytail and gold earring. Jesse stumbled to his feet and wiped his hand on his pants leg before reaching toward Eliot. When their fingers touched, I saw Eliot wince, ever so slightly. Then he gripped Jesse's hand firmly and shook it.

I shoved a chair away from the table with my foot and we invited Eliot to join us.

"I'll go get you a cup of coffee," I said. I rose from my chair and headed toward the counter. I stopped and turned back toward Eliot, staring at him helplessly. It had been so long since I'd offered him a cup of coffee, I couldn't remember . . .

Eliot looked at me and grinned. He'd read my mind. I looked into his eyes and as he smiled at me there was a tiny moment, just a flash, when his eyes were so filled with amusement and love that the pain had disappeared. "Black," he said. "I take it black."

I snapped my fingers. "That's right, black."

THAT night as I tucked Shelly into bed, I noticed she'd been crying. I sat on the edge of her bed and stroked my fingers through her golden hair. "What's wrong?" I said.

"Mom," she said, timidly, "how do you get boys to like you?"

I looked into her face and sighed. Would it never end? And would it do any good to tell her? I twisted a strand of her hair around my finger. "Shelly, sometimes when we want others to like us we try to be what we think they want us to be. We're afraid to be ourselves."

She nodded her head.

"Is there someone special you want to like you?"

She nodded again.

"Trying to get others to love us can make us feel desperate and insecure. God has promised to give us power to love others, but he hasn't given us a guarantee they will love us back. We can save ourselves a lot of frustration by concentrating on giving love rather than on getting it."

She drew her eyebrows together and stared at the ceiling, her smooth white forehead creased with tiny furrows. "That's kind of what God does, isn't it?" she said.

I stared into her beautiful young face and my eyes filled with tears. "Yes, Shelly," I said. "That's kind of what God does."

ELIOT was just closing the door to our bedroom when Tyler popped back into the hall.

"I want a drink of water," he said.

Eliot glanced at me and rolled his eyes to the ceiling. I was already in bed, holding the blankets around my naked shoulders.

"Well, hurry up," he said to Tyler.

Tyler dashed down the stairs, got his drink and ran back up the stairs and into his room. He popped his head back out the door. "Good night, Dad."

"Good night, Tyler."

Eliot closed our bedroom door.

WE were two lonely, hungry people. The ancient ritual was punctuated by laughter and cleansed by tears as we came together in a proclamation of love and commitment.

Afterward Eliot nestled his head close to my neck. "It seems we've met somewhere," he said. "What was your name?"

"Rebecca," I said. "Rebecca Adamson."

He snuggled closer. "Adamson, you say. You're sure it isn't Lorimer?"

"Nope. Adamson. I'm sure."

Eliot chuckled in satisfaction. "I think maybe things are getting back to the way they were," he said.

I started giggling. At first they were tiny little snickers coming from somewhere deep inside. But they grew until I was choking on my own laughter and I felt like I would never stop.

Eliot pulled away from me. "What's so funny?" he said.

I laughed and laughed, my head back on the pillow, my hands clasped against my breast.

"Rebecca," Eliot said, starting to laugh himself, "what's so funny, huh? What's so funny?" He started to laugh with me and then stopped because he didn't know what he was laughing at.

I tried to talk, but I was laughing too hard.

He laughed and then stopped again. "Rebecca, what is it? Did I say something funny?" He scratched his head and repeated his words, "I think things are getting back to the way they were. What's so funny about that?"

I went into a fresh gale of laughter. I tried to speak again, but when I couldn't get control of myself, I slipped my leg toward the edge of the bed and stuck my foot out from under the covers.

"My black socks," Eliot screamed, yanking back the covers to check my other foot. "You're wearing my black socks." He was aghast. "You made love to me while wearing my black socks!" Then Eliot threw back his head and cackled. "I don't believe you," he said. "I just don't believe you." He gathered me in his arms and we rocked back and forth, laughing and holding each other.

I sat up, holding the sheet around myself, and removed the black socks. I couldn't stand even the feel of their blackness against my pale legs a moment longer.

Eliot sat up also. I glanced at him and grinned.

"Well," he said, scratching his head and chuckling, "I guess things won't ever get back to exactly the way they were, will they?"

The remnants of laughter and passion still sparked in his serious eyes.

"Are you sorry?" I asked.

He shook his head from side to side.

I looked into his eyes—searching through the tiny red flashes of passion, the hint of pain, and the remnants of laughter.

"No," he said. "I'm not sorry. I'm glad."

I nodded. "So am I."